D1573849

Gage jumped to a sidewalk near the restaurant. He was shielded so no one could see him and then, as he walked down the street, he dropped the shield.

The evening was a beautiful summer evening in what used to be called the Rose City. In this area of town a number of cafes had tables and chairs outside on the sidewalk and they were filled with people talking and laughing.

One thing for sure about surviving something like the Event, it made the people of this planet very cheerful and looking to enjoy life. All of them had lost loved ones and family and knew they were lucky to be alive and rebuilding.

He had a date with a beautiful woman. One of the smartest and bravest women he had ever had the chance to meet. He had a hunch Angie was the right kind of woman now that she was being recruited to be a Seeder.

If he didn't blow this.

In all his life he had never been this confused about anything. And excited at the same time that he could be honest with Angie Park. He just had to hope she didn't end up hating him for being an alien.

A human alien, but still an alien.

STAR MIST

ALSO BY DEAN WESLEY SMITH

THE SEEDERS UNIVERSE

Dust and Kisses: A Seeders Universe Prequel Novel

Against Time

Sector Justice

Morning Song

The High Edge

Star Mist

Star Rain

Star Fall

Starburst

Rescue Two

STAR MIST

A SEEDERS UNIVERSE NOVEL

DEAN WESLEY SMITH

WMG PUBLISHING

Star Mist
Copyright © 2022 by Dean Wesley Smith
Published in a different form in *Smith's Monthly #25*, October, 2015
Published by WMG Publishing
Cover and Layout copyright © 2022 by WMG Publishing
Cover design by Allyson Longueira/WMG Publishing
Cover art copyright © Philcold | Dreamstime
ISBN-13: 978-1-56146-744-0
ISBN-10: 1-56146-744-8

This book is licensed for your personal enjoyment only. All rights reserved. This is a work of fiction. All characters and events portrayed in this book are fictional, and any resemblance to real people or incidents is purely coincidental. This book, or parts thereof, may not be reproduced in any form without permission.

For Kris

SECTION ONE
THE BEGINNING BEFORE THE BEGINNING

PROLOGUE

The alien ship looked more like a large pile of black and gray garbage smashed together into a large ball than a spaceship hanging there in the blackness of space just beyond the edge of the Milky Way Galaxy.

Yet Chairman Wade Ray knew it was a ship.

And that ship was the most important discovery in hundreds and hundreds of thousands of years of human history.

Chairman Wade Ray stood, his hands behind his back, in the command center of his ship, staring at the image of the alien ship on the huge monitor that filled one wall of the command center. Ray had his long, silver-gray hair pulled back as always and wore a dark-silk dress shirt and dark slacks and soft leather shoes.

He could feel the tension around him in the huge room like a heavy blanket on a warm night.

Sixteen people manned stations behind him and not a one could be heard. They all felt as he felt, that what they were seeing couldn't be possible.

Tacita, his wife and partner and co-chairman of this ship, stood beside him, also just studying the strange shape of the alien ship. She had her hair extremely short and wore a black silk pantsuit.

To Ray, she was the most beautiful woman he had ever seen and he had been in love with her for more years than he wanted to think about.

He couldn't imagine ever not having her brilliant mind and sharp wit working beside him.

Especially now, when they faced an alien ship.

He shook his head. How was this even possible?

No alien race in thousands and thousands of galaxies had ever managed to survive long enough to build even a galaxy-wide civilization, let alone a ship that could travel the vast distances between galaxies. When the Seeder scout ships discover an alien race growing on any planet in a galaxy, at any level, the Seeders would just go around that galaxy.

Over the centuries, Seeder research ships would watch the alien development, but never interfere. It was one of their most scared laws, learned out of bad experience a long, long time ago.

Very few alien races even survived long enough to make it off their own planet. And even fewer found trans-tunnel drive to jump to other close stars. And for as long as humans had been seeding galaxies with more humans, no alien race had found the refinements to trans-tunnel drives to get the standard speeds to break out of their own limited galaxies.

Yet somehow, he was looking at an alien ship that was between galaxies.

And moving at standard trans-tunnel drive speeds.

"Any life signs at all of any type?" Tacita asked.

"Nothing," Commander Chain said. "We also checked for any form of stasis. Nothing."

Chain was their most trusted second in command on any ship and had been with them thousands of years. He looked, as most Seeders looked, to be about thirty. He had dark brown hair and never was seen out of jeans and a sweatshirt.

"How large is that ship?" Ray asked.

"The size of a Seeder mother ship," Chain said.

Seeder mother ships were the largest ships Seeder's built. Mother ships were the size of small moons and shaped like birds gliding. They could hold a thousand other ships and upwards of a million people comfortably.

"Any equipment at all active?" Tacita asked.

"Except for the trans-tunnel drive still powering it forward," Chain said. "Nothing is active. No atmosphere of any kind, no readings other than the drive. And honestly, it looks like the drive is about to fail as well."

"Can you get a reading on the age?" Ray asked.

"At least two hundred thousand standard years," Chase said. "And from the looks of the damage from impacts of small particles and such after its shields failed, it has been dead for a good hundred thousand of those years."

"Trace back its flight path and put up on the screen where it came from," Tacita said.

Ray was surprised when the image appeared of a thousand galaxies in all their various groupings. Right now they were in the middle of what was called the "Local Cluster" by humans in this galaxy. About thirty galaxies of different sizes and shapes. On the scale on the map on the screen, the local cluster barely showed up as a dot.

The alien ship had originated, or passed through a galaxy that was a vast distance away. Ray guessed there were four hundred galaxies between where it started and where it was now.

"I've accounted for galactic movement on the rough track," Chase said. "That ship never got near another galaxy of any size since it left that galaxy."

"At its speed," Ray asked, "was the ship still functioning when it left that galaxy?"

"Yes," Chase said. "From what we can gather on preliminary scans, it appears it left that galaxy very much alive and functioning."

A dot appeared about halfway along the line of travel on the big screen. "The ship went dead about at this point, from what we can tell so far."

"We need a massive amount of study of this ship," Tacita said. "To find out who this race was and what happened to this ship."

She looked at Ray and he nodded.

Ray agreed completely. They did need a massive amount of study on this ship. And they were going to have to do it carefully and not miss anything.

But his eye went back along the line the ship had taken from that original galaxy. They also needed to know what was happening there and in the galaxies around it.

Two hundred thousand years had passed. Were these aliens expanding as humans did?

And were they warlike?

In space where very, very few advanced civilizations ever emerged from planets, what would the aliens even think if they knew humans were here and spread over hundreds of thousands of galaxies in this area?

Ray kept staring at the image of the ship's path on the wall screen.

Even by the galaxy-spanning scale Seeders worked and

thought at, the alien original galaxy was a very, very long distance away.

CHAPTER 1

Angie Park let the sounds of her motorcycle die off into the silence of the forest and the ruins around her. Nothing moved, not even a slight breeze among the tall pines and the deserted general store and gas station tucked back into the trees.

The building had been cute at one point in the past, almost like a cottage, but now the paint was peeling, the windows were covered in grime, and weeds were growing thick between the building and the useless gas pump. On one side blackberries were starting to crawl up a wall and in a few years would bury the old building.

She had parked on the edge of the two-lane road that wound up through the Cascade Mountains. The road in this area had been still in good shape and very few car wrecks had blocked her for the last twenty miles since she had left I-5.

She pulled off her helmet and let her long black hair fall over her shoulders as she dismounted and set the helmet on her leather supply pack. She was thin and tall and had no trouble at all on the large road bikes.

She had a small saddle rifle in a sling on her back and a small caliber gun hidden in a holster on her leg under her jeans.

Her light jacket covered a T-shirt and she unzipped the jacket to let in the fresh mountain air. It was early summer and the heat today was predicted to be around ninety by the middle of the afternoon, even this high in the mountains.

Around her the silence of the Oregon forest seemed to press in, but after all the years of being alone, she was used to silence more than the noise of being around other people. That's why she had volunteered for this task, to go out and tell others about Portland.

Plus she really believed in what Portland was building and wanted everyone to know.

Up a small dirt road in front of her that wound through the tall pine trees, she knew a compound sat at the top of that road with six people living in it. Six survivors of the Event, as it was now being called.

The Event had been a wave of electromagnetic energy that swept over the Earth just over three years ago. It hadn't hurt equipment, but it had killed any exposed humans and dogs and horses and a few other animals. Thankfully it spared cats because she didn't know what she would have done the first few years of being alone without her cats to keep her company.

Humans who had survived were like her. They happened to be underground or in a vault of some type and were protected from the invisible but deadly wave. She had been a Professor of Physics at the University of Oregon and had been three stories down in a lab under the physics department when the Event happened. Millions like her had survived worldwide, and now civilization was working to rebuild.

After the Event, she had moved far up the Columbia Gorge in a home overlooking the river to get away from all the smell of decaying bodies. She had discovered that civilization was rebuilding when convoy after convoy of motorcycles went down the freeway below her home headed for Portland in the spring of the second year. Men, women, and children.

Because of its climate and natural resources, Portland had been picked as one of the five cities to be the center of the new world in this country. She had followed the convoys after a time and saw and listened to what they were doing and trying to build. A month later she had packed up her cats and moved to Portland to try to help.

Now she was doing what they called "outreach" to those who hadn't heard yet about building the new world. It was dangerous, but she had wanted to do it. A couple of her friends had insisted she not go alone, but she had felt that a woman alone would be more convincing than a bunch of people. So far, she had been right about that.

Since so many of the military had survived on ships, submarines, underground compounds, all the top science had survived as well and was being used in the rebuild. She had seen satellite photos of the compound at the end of the dirt road that was her next stop for the day.

She knew that six were living there. They had set up electrical and had running water to most of their buildings and had a pretty decent surveillance system set up that more than likely was watching her now.

That's why she had stopped here, to let them watch her. Last thing she needed to do was surprise anyone who had been surviving and living off of nature for three years. Doing that could get a person really dead really quickly.

Over the years, it seemed that a lot of people had gone completely insane thinking that civilization was gone and that they were left alone.

She had thought at one point she might go insane as well because death was just everywhere. The very reason she had found a place on the top of a hill was for protection from the nut cases roaming around, and to avoid the smell of death that first year. But she had set that home up so she could protect it. Luckily, she never had had to.

She looked up the dirt road that wound into the tall pines. It looked far cooler than where she was standing now near the highway in the sun. She needed to get moving.

She knew the names of four of the six people who were living there. And knew that two of them had surviving family members.

Of the thirty compounds like this one she had approached over the last six months, most had come into the city later on their own terms to see what was going on, and after that, many had moved into town just as she had done.

But others were happy where they were and she respected that.

Her job wasn't to convince them to join humanity again, but to just let them know what was happening.

She took a long cool drink from her canteen, put it back on her bike, then with her hands in the air, started up the road toward the compound. Walking like that told the people watching she knew she was being watched and only wanted to talk.

At least she hoped that's what it told them.

CHAPTER 2

"Oh, no, Angie," Gage Teal said to himself from his apartment living room computer station. "Don't go in there alone. Those folks are whack jobs."

On the screen he saw Angie Park raise her hands above her head and start up the dirt road toward the compound.

"Shit, just shit," Gage said, jamming his feet into his shoes and using his comm link to call his three-member team. She had talked herself out of other tough spots, but from his recon on the people in this compound, there was no talking her way out of this one. The people there were nut jobs and cold-blooded killers.

"Situation," he said to his team when all three answered. "Emergency. Meet me in the staging room in one minute max."

This was what they had all trained for and had done a few times. But his sole person to take care of was Angie Park and right now she was within minutes of being shot.

He finished getting on his shoes and then looked back at the screen. She was almost up the dirt road to the compound.

He had watched her for six months from one of the many shielded Seeder ships in orbit, making sure that she was safe. She was a very special person and the more he had watched her, the more he had come to realize that.

She was special to the Seeders for some reason he didn't know. And she was sometimes foolishly brave. He had fallen for her.

And he had never even met her.

Looked like that was about to change very quickly.

He teleported to the staging room and was the second one there. Only Drake, his second in command for the unit, had arrived ahead of Gage.

Drake looked almost square, with a thick neck and a very wide forehead. He was married to the nicest woman on the planet who was so tiny, Drake could have snapped her in half with his bare hands. Gage didn't want to think about how they had managed two kids.

The staging room was a small room with a wall of weapons that looked like United States military weapons but were actually a bunch more. A large computer screen and a command console filled the other wall.

"Angie?" Drake asked as both of them grabbed their weapons of choice. Both carried what looked like standard issue military rifles and both strapped another gun on their hips in a holster. The rifles were actually laser and could kill or stun a person from a half mile away.

"She's about to walk into a mess," Gage said, pulling up the large screen as Jean Marsh and Rollie King appeared and moved to the gun wall. They were a couple and looked like twins instead of being married. Both were as tall as Gage at six foot, both wore body-shirts that made their intense muscle training show clearly.

Both wore their brown hair short and only Marsh pretended to break the mold with an earring on one ear.

But they loved to dress exactly the same to mess with people's minds at times. Clearly they had just come directly from a workout.

"What's Angie's walking into this time?" Drake asked.

They had jumped for Angie three times before and hadn't had to show themselves. But this time was bad, real bad.

Gage showed them the compound and the six people as they gathered around the big screen.

One person was staying in a cabin with a rifle, one was getting set as a sniper in a tree near the road, and the other three were waiting for Angie to come to them.

A sixth man had already gone down to the road and taken Angie's motorcycle and was pushing it up the dirt road.

"She's in deep this time," Marsh said, shaking her head.

"We stun and relocate," Gage said. "I'll clear the sniper and the guy with the bike, Marsh and King, you two take the three that will face Angie on the road. Drake, you take the one in the cabin. Wait for my mark."

All three of them nodded and each pointed to a spot they would jump to.

"Let's get into positions," Gage said.

Then he touched a key on the command table and said, "Four transporting to the surface."

"Clear," the answer came back.

They all teleported at once and a moment later Gage found himself in a small hidden area behind Angie where he could see the sniper and hear the conversation Angie was about to have.

The air felt warm, almost hot, and the smell of pine filled the air.

As he got ready and made sure his rifle was on stun, his team checked in that they were in position.

This wasn't the way he had hoped to meet Angie. But it looked like it was going to have to do.

If something didn't go wrong and she got killed. He would never forgive himself if that happened.

CHAPTER 3

It took her seven minutes to walk up the dirt road before she crested over a slight ridge. She was sweating and now wished she had brought along her canteen instead of leaving it on the bike. It wasn't much after ten in the morning and it was already getting hot.

And walking with her hands in the air was never an easy task, especially going uphill as she had been doing.

Ahead she could see the five buildings of the compound, all well-maintained. Three single-story houses and two tall-peaked barns sat in a cluster with some fenced-in chicken areas to one side. The fence on those were tall and strung between solid poles, more than likely in an attempt to keep out mountain lions that roamed these hills.

She kept her hands in the air and kept walking toward the compound.

After another hundred paces, a man and two women stepped

out of one house and moved to meet her. All three carried rifles, but had them cradled in their arms or down in one hand.

The woman on the right Angie recognized as Bettie Collins from photos. The woman on the left was her sister LeAnne. They had both lived in a small town to the east of here. She had no idea how they survived the Event. They must have been in a deep basement or something at the time as Angie had been.

The tall, very thin man in the middle Angie didn't recognize, but he looked to be about her age at thirty and had intelligence in his eyes that didn't seem to miss anything.

She instantly had a bad feeling about him.

Instantly.

That was unusual.

None of them seemed at all worried about meeting a stranger. That wasn't normal in these situations either.

All three of them were dressed in jeans, light shirts, and work boots and all their clothing looked new and clean.

As they got within ten steps, the three stopped and Bettie signaled for Angie to stop and she did.

She was about ten yards from the tree line and very much out in the open.

"Put your arms down," Bettie said. "That had to be hard walking like that."

Angie did, smiling and rubbing her shoulders. "I've done it numbers of times, but it never gets that much easier. I'm Angela Park, but everyone just calls me Angie."

"Everyone," the man asked, clearly puzzled and not introducing himself at all.

Angie nodded. "That's what I'm here to tell you about. Civilization is slowly rebuilding. Portland is one of the five cities picked to be one of the centers. I'm just out trying to inform everyone about what is happening."

"How many people are in Portland?" Bettie asked.

Angie shrugged. "Last count about forty thousand."

"Forty thousand," LeAnne said, breathlessly.

The man didn't even flinch.

Angie nodded. "And your Aunt Carol is there and knew I was coming out this way and told me to send her best wishes. She survived as well."

Angie thought both Bettie and LeAnne were going to collapse right there, but both managed to take deep breaths and then look at each other.

Angie was starting to feel that something was off here. She wasn't sure, but her little voice was starting to get worried. These people were not reacting in the way that survivors on their own normally reacted, which was usually with fear and then relief that civilization was rebuilding.

"Since civilization destroyed itself one time," the man said, "why is everyone so fired up to rebuild?"

"Humans had nothing to do with the Event," Angie said. "It was an electromagnetic wave that came out of deep space and swept over the entire planet. The scientists who knew it was coming thought it would be harmless. Turns out it was at a certain frequency that fried something in our human brains and everyone who wasn't either underground or protected behind steel died instantly and painlessly. It did not harm equipment."

"How do you know all this?" he asked.

"May I?" she asked, pointing to her back pocket.

He nodded and didn't raise his rifle.

He should have raised his rifle.

Something was very off.

As she pulled out three folded sheets and offered them to him, she glanced around looking for the three others who lived here to be in positions to kill her at the guy's signal. If they wanted to, she was as good as dead. She was a good ten running steps from the nearest shelter.

Bettie stepped forward and took the sheets, then stepped back and looked at the papers, handing them to the others one at a time.

"That information was recorded from the International Space Station," Angie said, staying on her practiced patter. "We finally got the men who were up there down a year ago, and used a couple existing rockets to resupply them in the meantime."

All three looked at each sheet. LeAnne held onto them when they were finished.

They had no questions at all.

Under normal circumstances, they would have questions. A lot of questions.

What the hell was going on here?

Angie took a deep breath and kept going. "The third sheet is a summary of what is happening in Portland and around the world, when the first major election will be for both Portland and the United States. And so on."

"Seems very civilized like," the man said.

Again Angie pointed to her pocket. "May I?"

The man nodded and Angie pulled out an iPhone and charging cord and a paper list and offered them.

Bettie again stepped forward and took the iPhone, charging cord, and paper.

Then she stepped back beside the man.

No comment about how useless it was, nothing. More than anything Angie wanted to just turn and run, but more than likely if she did that she would be cut down from the hidden guns of the others.

"Cell towers are now working along the Interstate Five route from Portland down to Eugene and all around the Portland area," Angie said. "That's a list of numbers you can call for more information if you go down near the freeway. And your aunt's number is on there as well."

Nothing.

Not one bit of comment at all.

Angie had every alarm bell in her body going off. She had to get out of there and get going now!

She smiled. "Nice chatting with all of you. I hope you decide to stop into the city when you get a chance. It's very nice."

She raised her hands and stepped backwards.

"I don't think you'll be leaving just yet," the man said, bringing his rifle up and aiming at her.

LeAnne and Bettie did the same.

Behind her, she heard a man huffing. She glanced over her shoulder to see a man pushing her bike up the road. "This is a nice ride," he said as he got over the crest of the small rise.

"What's going on here?" she asked.

"We never allow visitors to leave once they know we are here," the man said.

"We have to protect ourselves," Bettie said.

"We are so sorry," LeAnne said.

But to Angie she didn't look sorry at all. More than likely numbers of people had stumbled into this place and were buried in back somewhere, which is where she was about to end up.

Why had she ever thought she could do this job alone?

CHAPTER 4

Gage listened to the conversation Angie was having with the three and then the stunned and worried sound of her voice when the guy with her bike came up behind her.

"Stand ready," Gage said to his team through their comm links. "And Marsh and King, back me on the guy with the bike in case I can't get a clear shot."

"Copy," Marsh said.

He watched Angie stand there, facing almost certain death, staying calm and proud. She was an amazing woman and when this was over, it was time he finally got to know her.

He had an apartment in Portland to be part of the team there when needed. In fact, all of them did. And each of them protected a certain Seeder-important person in town. In fact, if his team ever took a name, it would be Guardian Angels.

Marsh and King were assigned to watch over a couple by the name of Carey Noack and Matt Ladel. They had actually become friends with them without ever telling Carey or Matt that they were being guarded. And Carey and Matt didn't know about the Seeders ships in orbit or the vast human society that covered the galaxy and far beyond.

But for some reason, those higher in the Seeders considered Carey and Matt worth protecting, along with Angie, who didn't know about the Seeders either.

Drake had been assigned to watch and protect Benny Slade. Benny and his girlfriend were already Seeders, but they had elected to remain on the planet and unknown to Benny and his girlfriend, Drake was watching out for them.

The team had not had to be called for a problem with anyone but Angie. Gage had a hunch that Angie wouldn't stop doing her job until someone told her about the Seeders. And Gage had no idea when that would be.

So he stood ready to take out the sniper from the tree and the guy with her motorcycle the moment it looked like Angie's talking could no longer save the day.

She was one brave person, going out and doing this alone. Wow.

CHAPTER 5

"I am no threat to you," Angie said. "All we wanted to do was tell you about what was happening. You are free to stay here for the rest of your lives. No one cares."

"Someone always cares," the man said.

The two women nodded. Both of them looked very pained. Clearly the year after the Event had not gone well for them.

The man pushing the bike had stopped behind her about ten steps right at the tree line. She had no doubt, without looking, that he had a gun trained on her as well.

If these people were so worried about being found, maybe Angie had one last thing to say to save her life.

"If you allow me to leave here," Angie said, "I will just cross this compound off as not interested."

"I am sure you would," the man said.

"But if you kill me, if anything happens to me, the new government will come swooping in here faster than you can ever imagine. Murder is still murder in a civilized world."

"No one knows where you are at," the man said, laughing. "You're just like those religious types who used to bang on doors back when the world was still alive. You just want us to follow you to your church so you can take our things."

"Check the bag on my bike," Angie said, staring at the man. "There are satellite images of this compound that were taken just recently. They are watching us now as I speak because they knew I was going to be here. You think I am stupid enough to walk in here alone?"

She was damn proud of herself that her voice didn't shake when she said that, even though she had been just as stupid as she claimed not to be.

The man nodded and behind Angie she could hear the other guy rummaging in her pack. He pulled out the photos of this compound and let out a small gasp. Then he let the bike drop and moved around Angie to hand the images to the man between LeAnne and Bettie.

The man looked at them and suddenly didn't seem so sure of himself.

"So go ahead and shoot me," Angie said. "But expect the helicopters and police to descend on this compound in less than two hours. But you let me go, I just cross this place off as you not being interested and you can go on with your lives for as long as you want."

"I think you are bluffing," the man said.

"Look at the photo," she said, actually bluffing her socks off. "Can you tell when it was taken? I left Portland two days ago with it. They took it for me so I would know what they were watching and so I could find this place easily. You are my third stop. They watch me closely at every stop."

The man looked at the photo, then simply tore it up and dropped it on the ground.

"We let you leave and for sure you tell everyone about us. We kill you and take the chance that you weren't being watched. I think we'll go with that second chance."

He raised his gun and at that moment all four of them just slumped to the ground. And there was a crashing beside the road and another woman slumped out of a tree and fell to the ground.

What the hell was going on?

She stood there staring at the four bodies in front of her, letting her racing heart slow just a little. She had been seconds away from being very dead.

Very, very dead.

What had happened?

At that moment, a man came walking up the road, smiling at her. "Bet you thought you were bluffing, didn't you?"

She opened her mouth to say something, then just shut it.

The guy walking toward her had a smile that lit up his face and a body that would turn any head. He looked to be about six-feet tall, with wide shoulders and short, dark hair. His skin looked smooth and tan, as if he spent a lot of time in the sun. He wore jeans, a dark green T-shirt, and had a gun on his hip in a holster that just looked like it belonged there.

"Angie, sorry we had to finally meet like this," he said, extending his hand.

She took his calm, dry hand in her sweaty hand and shook it, still stunned beyond words as to what had happened.

"I'm Lieutenant Gage Teal. Former United States Special Forces. I've been in charge of your protection detail for the last six months."

"Holy shit," she said, almost gasping for air. "You just saved my life."

"And that's exactly why we have been watching you all along," he said, smiling. "Me and my team always went in ahead of your scheduled stop to make sure you got the protection you needed."

"Thank you," she said, not really knowing what to think other than that she was still alive and the man responsible could be a Greek God. Wearing a damn T-shirt that showed muscles no human should ever have.

"I thought you were going to talk your way out of this mess as well," he said. "You had the nutball thinking there for a while."

She laughed. "Desperation brings on wild stories. I just didn't know any of them were true."

"Ninety-nine percent of the time," he said, "it is better to think you are alone when facing these survivors. Glad we were here for that one percent."

"Yeah," Angie said, "me, too." She was still trying to catch her breath. Near-death experiences can make you real short of breath it seemed.

"Can you help me get these people rounded up? My men have spread out to scout the area to make sure no one else is around."

"Are they dead?" Angie asked. "And what kind of weapon was that?"

"A ray gun, actually," he said, laughing "sort of along the same principle as the wave that killed in the Event, only not fatal. Just knocks a person out for a few hours and gives them a real nasty headache."

"Good," she said, laughing.

"The fifth one fell out of a tree over here where we stunned her," he said, moving off to the right.

They each took one of the woman's arms and dragged her back to the others in the middle of the road. She was about Angie's age—around thirty—and also looked as clean and fresh as the others. But clearly the Event and this leader guy had really twisted their minds and made them into killers.

"Where is the sixth one?" she asked after they got the woman near the others.

"In the big house," he said. "We can leave her there for the pickup."

"What are you going to do with them?" she asked.

"Helicopter will take them down into the old Central America and dump them off with enough water and food to survive for a few days. It's pretty wild down there still. Perfect for their type. What they manage to do from there is their business."

She laughed. "I love that. Serves the creeps right."

He walked her back to her bike and helped her get it upright again. Her helmet must still be down near the highway.

She secured her bag on her bike and then turned to look at him. Damn, he had green eyes.

She loved green eyes.

Now she wasn't sure if her heart was still racing from almost being killed or racing because the man standing next to her was so damn good-looking.

How was it possible that the man who had saved her ass was handsome and had green eyes?

"How about from now on out we do this as a team?" she asked.

"We have been a team since you went out the first time," he said, smiling. "You just didn't know it."

"How about you and I work together then, so I know your

plans and I don't go off course and change plans on you and get myself killed in some place you can't rescue my skinny ass?"

He laughed. "I like that a lot. So what are your plans next?"

"I'm going back to Portland to my wonderful house and my two cats, take a long, cool bath, and try to stop shaking."

He nodded, the smile still on his face.

"After that I am going to go out and have a nice dinner at a nice restaurant and a few drinks to try to bury the memory of these nut cases."

"Would you like company for dinner and a few drinks?" he asked.

"I would love that," she said. "Do you know where I live?"

She wasn't sure that she wanted to know the answer to that, but she had asked anyway.

"Not a clue," he said.

"Northwest sector of town," she said. "You ever heard of a restaurant called Danny's in the Pearl area?"

"Best chicken and pizza in all of Portland," he said, his smile lighting up an already hot and bright day.

"Six p.m.," she said, climbing on her bike and firing it up.

"Six p.m.," he said, nodding to her.

She turned her bike and headed slowly down the dirt road, not daring to look at the lieutenant behind her.

She had almost died, been rescued by the most handsome man left on the planet, and now she had a date with him.

If he had come in on a white horse it wouldn't have made it any stranger, other than the fact that horses had been killed in the Event as well.

Who knew that facing down crazy survivalists could get her a date.

It was a strange damn world, of that there was no doubt.

And she was going to enjoy every minute of still being alive, and maybe later, every inch of the body of the man who saved her.

A girl could hope.

CHAPTER 6

"Got a date, huh?" Drake said as he came around the end of the house dragging the woman who had been inside through the dust like she was so much luggage.

"Figured it was the best way," Gage said, smiling, really, really happy that Angie had said yes to meeting him.

"So we were scouting, huh?" Marsh said, appearing out of the tree line twenty steps to the right. King appeared at the same time on the left.

"Easier to just let her get on the road again," Gage said.

"Sure, sure," Marsh said, shaking her head.

Drake dropped the unconscious woman in the pile of other human garbage. "So what exactly are we doing with these sickos?"

"I'll have transport drop them with some supplies on a beach in Central America a very long distance from any other humans. Not my issue if they survive or not, but they will be alone like they wanted. They just won't have anyone but each other to kill."

"Perfect," Drake said.

"Call us if you need backup on this date," Marsh said, smiling at Gage.

"Don't call me," Drake said. "My wife and I are having dinner with my charges tonight in Portland. We're going to tell them we are Seeders as well."

"But not that you have been guarding them?" Gage asked, surprised.

"Nope," Drake said. "We like them as friends and just figured we could expand the menu for meals some if they knew who we really were."

Gage laughed. "Real good point."

"Wish we could tell Carey and Matt," Marsh said. "We like them as well."

"I have a hunch the reason we are all doing this guarding will come clear sooner rather than later," Gage said.

"You know something we don't?" Marsh asked.

"Just a gut sense," Gage said. "When I report how close Angie came to being killed today, movement might just happen."

"Yeah," Drake said. "Real good point. Now can we get out of this heat?"

With that, Gage touched his ear. "Four transporting on board."

"Clear," came the response.

And a moment later they were back putting their weapons away. Gage jumped back to his apartment after thanking his team and wrote his report and submitted it.

Then he headed for the shower, whistling, after spending an hour watching Angie ride into Portland to make sure that she got safely to her apartment.

He had a date with a beautiful and courageous woman. It didn't get any better than that.

CHAPTER 7

Angie lay in her tub in her wonderful apartment, just letting the water calm her and take away the shaking.

Well, at least attempt to take away the shaking. She had never had this kind of reaction before to an event. But she had never gotten within a second of sure death before either.

When she got home, she had forced herself to make a sandwich and eat it before taking a bath. The food and the warm water were helping, but still every time she thought about how close she had come to dying today, she started shaking again.

She was getting annoyed at it and also annoyed that her shaking was making water slosh out of the tub.

Finally, she drained the water and took a very cold shower and then washed her long black hair. The day was warm enough it would dry before her dinner date.

And doing such a regular thing and the cold water finally got the shakes stopped.

She couldn't believe that a handsome man had just shown up,

saved her life, and then arranged to have a date with her. That was a very, very goofy thing.

Except for the part that he had saved her life.

And that he was scary handsome.

All she really wanted to do was touch those muscles under his T-shirt to see if they were for real. He looked to be about her age at thirty, but she had never met a man in that kind of shape at that age before. Clearly they existed.

What she didn't realize was that those stun weapons they had used existed. Especially done in a way so that they looked like regular-issue rifles. That seemed pretty advanced, especially only three years after the Event.

There was an awful lot about the handsome stranger who had saved her life that she wanted to know.

She checked the time. She needed to get dressed and get going on the four-block walk down to the restaurant.

This would be a very interesting dinner. Not only because he was so handsome and had green eyes and muscles that wouldn't stop, but because she wanted to know exactly how he had followed her for six months without her knowing it.

And where those stun weapons came from.

And if he had a girlfriend.

CHAPTER 8

Chairman Soma asked Gage to report to his office at once just forty minutes before he was to transport to the planet for the date with Angie.

Gage and his team were stationed on the Seeders ship *Home Stand* that was one of five shielded ships in orbit over this planet to try to help it rebuild from a devastating hit by an electromagnetic wave. Thousands of Seeders were implanted in communities around the globe to help in the rebuilding.

But in almost a year being on this ship, Gage had not had a chance to meet Chairman Soma.

Every Seeder ship was its own business that worked to make a profit and continue, thus what would be called the captain was called the chairman. Gage knew what he was getting for his guard duty was very high pay, so for some reason this planet out of all the other human planets in this galaxy was special.

You didn't often see five Seeder ships in orbit around any

planet for any reason, especially planets that hadn't advanced far enough yet to join the larger group of planets.

Gage had a hunch his report today was what caused this sudden meeting with the chairman.

Gage finished putting on his tennis shoes and transported to the chairman's office.

The room was huge, with a large oak-colored wooden desk, soft brown carpet, pictures of various planets and star-groups on the walls in oranges and reds. There was a large brown cloth couch and a few large chairs that matched.

The room felt comfortable and lived-in.

As he arrived, Chairman Soma stood from one of the chairs and extended his hand. "Great job today keeping Angie Park alive."

"That's what I am assigned to do," Gage said.

Captain Soma was a solid man, with huge shoulders and no gut at all. He looked like he could pick a couch up off the floor with one hand. He had short-cut brown hair and dark, penetrating eyes. He wore what looked like sweat pants and a massive body shirt and no shoes.

Another man stood from a second chair. The other man was tall and had very long silver hair. He wore a silk shirt and dark pants and just radiated power and intelligence.

Soma turned and said, "Gage Teal, I would like you to meet Chairman Wade Ray."

Gage shook his hand and said, "Nice meeting you."

"Actually," Ray said, "the pleasure is mine."

Then Gage's brain kicked in and he realized who he had just met was the legend of all Seeders, maybe the oldest human alive. He was rumored to be hundreds of thousands of years old.

Gage started to open his mouth to say something but not a damn thought came to his mind to say.

The two chairmen indicated that Gage should take a seat on the couch and he did.

Chairman Ray got right to the point. "We think it's time to bring in Angie Park and tell her about us."

Of all the things either of these men could have said, that was the biggest surprise. And it finally explained why he and his team had been guarding her for all this time.

"She has Seeder genes?"

Both men nodded.

"She is very special," Ray said, "and so are you and four others in this area of this planet."

Again Gage opened his mouth to say something, but then realized that the greatest human to have ever lived had just called him special.

Ray just smiled as Gage managed to get some sort of sense of thought back in control. Ray would not be here if there wasn't a need for some mission and since he had just called him special along with the others on the surface, that meant that whatever quality they all had was needed for something very important.

He had been around the military part of the Seeders for a few hundred years now and he knew that was how it worked.

"I assume you have a mission for us," Gage said, "meaning me and the other five still on the planet. And whatever makes us special is the key to this mission."

Ray glanced at Soma who just smiled and shook his head.

"We do," Ray said. "And yes, you are correct. But if you wouldn't mind, I would like to explain it all to everyone at the same time."

Gage understood that completely and nodded. "So what do you need me to do?"

"You know Angie Park as well as anyone, since you have been tracking her," Ray said. "Figure out a way to introduce the fact that this ship is here and what Seeders actually are."

Gage nodded. "I have a date with her in exactly ten minutes. How long do I have?"

"As soon as possible," Ray said. "A few days at most."

"And the others I assume are the ones my team has also been protecting?"

"They are," Ray said. "Two are already Seeders and will be bringing along the other two."

"What about my team?" Gage asked.

"They will be going with you on your mission if you want them, and they agree to it, as you must do as well."

Gage nodded and stood.

The other two men stood and both shook his hand.

Chairman Soma said, "Report to me your progress and I will keep Chairman Ray updated."

"And enjoy the date," Ray said, smiling.

"I will," Gage said and then jumped back to his apartment on the ship, splashed some water on his face to try to get his mind working, and then told command that he was jumping to the planet.

"Clear," the command voice came back.

A moment later he jumped to a sidewalk near the restaurant. He was shielded so no one could see him and then, as he walked down the street, he dropped the shield.

The evening was a beautiful summer evening in what used to be called the Rose City. The air had a freshness to it and a slight breeze kept the air comfortable. In this area of town a number of cafes had tables and chairs outside on the sidewalk and they were filled with people talking and laughing.

One thing for sure about surviving something like the Event, it made the people of this planet very cheerful and looking to enjoy life. All of them had lost loved ones and family and knew they were lucky to be alive and rebuilding.

He had a date with a beautiful woman. One of the smartest and bravest women he had ever had the chance to meet. It had been a very long time for him, maybe almost eighty years since he and his first and so far only wife had decided to go their own ways. They still loved each other, but just had very different interests.

He had a few one-night stands out of bars over the years, but his job kept him busy and not really meeting the right kind of women.

He had a hunch Angie was the right kind of woman now that she was being recruited to be a Seeder.

If he didn't blow this.

And why he and Angie were special to someone like Chairman Wade Ray was beyond him.

In all his life he had never been this confused about anything.

And excited at the same time that he could be honest with Angie Park.

He just had to hope she didn't end up hating him for being an alien.

A human alien, but still an alien.

CHAPTER 9

Angie stood just outside the restaurant watching for Gage Teal. There was no chance in hell she was going to go inside, get a table, and then sit there alone if he stood her up.

Or if she had just been imagining all that this afternoon.

The evening was flat perfect, with a cool breeze off the river and the temperature in the mid-seventies. She had decided to just go with her normal way of dressing in jeans, but had put on her best new blue blouse and some pearl earrings that had been her mother's.

Angie felt dressed up. And that was all that mattered.

Then suddenly there he was, walking toward her down the sidewalk. He also had on jeans, tennis shoes, and a white dress shirt with the sleeves rolled up. He saw her and broke into the same smile she had seen up in the mountains earlier after he had saved her life.

And that smile almost melted her right there on the sidewalk.

"Sorry I am slightly late," he said as he came up to her. "A meeting with some top brass."

"Only just got here myself," she said, smiling back at him and those intense green eyes.

God, if she wasn't careful, she might just stare into those eyes all night and not say a word.

"Hungry?" he asked, indicating the restaurant they were in front of that smelled wonderful.

The smell was a mixture of garlic and pasta and fresh-baked bread. This place was also known for the best pizza in town and chicken in an Italian sauce that could melt in a person's mouth. After getting here, the smell of garlic and pizza had made her decide that was what she was going to have.

"Famished," she said. "Almost being killed can do that for a girl."

He laughed as she turned to lead the way inside and damn if she didn't love the sound of his laugh as well.

It was going to be everything she could do to just not jump him right here in the restaurant. She realized this afternoon that she hadn't had a date since the Event. For some reason she had just never met a person she wanted to date amid all the death. But now that life was returning to at least Portland and a few other cities around the world, she was beyond ready.

Also during the first part of the last few years, her focus had been on staying alive and then helping in the recovery. But she had never been the celibate type before the Event. While working on her Doctorate in Physics, she had even been engaged. But they had both been too busy and that had broken off.

And after she became a professor, all the men just looked too young for her, even though she wasn't much older than most of them.

Of course, even when she was dating, she just knew she sucked at long-term relationships. Just sucked.

But now she had a date and if she didn't screw this up, it might be something worthwhile for some great sex for a few months.

They managed to get a table in the back corner of the restaurant. The table was wood with a red tablecloth on it and the chairs were solid and also wood. A couple tall plants divided their table from the nearest one and gave them some privacy, which she liked.

A waiter named Bud took their drink order and left them staring at each other.

"I am so glad I finally get a chance to meet and talk with you," Gage said.

"I'm glad you and I can talk as well," she said, smiling at him. "If you hadn't been shadowing me this morning I wouldn't be here."

He just shrugged, which she loved. "Just doing my job."

"And who hired you to do this job?" she asked. "And why me?"

"Honestly," he said, "those are the two toughest questions you could have asked and I will tell you the truth on both a little later, except I honestly don't know why you."

Then she watched as he laughed. "And to be honest, I don't know why me and my team either. So I'm hoping together we can get some answers as to why both of us ended up in that compound this morning."

She frowned. She had not expected that kind of answer at all. She wasn't sure what she had been expecting, but it wasn't that.

"How about we get to know each other a little first," he asked. "What did you do before the Event? Were you married or engaged and if either of those questions are too personal, tell me to mind my own business."

She laughed and the worry in his eyes dropped away.

"You sure you want to know?" she asked.

"Very much," he said, nodding.

"Not married and no boyfriend before the Event and I was a professor of physics."

He sat back with that, clearly thinking for a moment. Then he said, "That's cool."

"That I didn't have a boyfriend?" she asked, smiling at him and he laughed.

"No, the physics part," he said, "but glad you didn't lose a loved one as well."

She looked into those green eyes. Did she really want to know this man's background or not. Finally she decided she did. "And you?"

"Pretty close to your expertise, actually," he said. "I have a doctorate in mathematics."

That rocked her back. God, he was smart and handsome.

Holy shit.

"In fact," he said, "all four members of my team have higher degrees in one thing or another."

She shook her head and he laughed.

"Military image doesn't often cover higher degrees, does it? Does that make you want to stop this dinner?"

She laughed and said, "Oh, I think I can put up with someone who is smart for at least the length of a dinner. So that education scares off women, does it?"

He shrugged and took a piece of bread from a basket that had just been dropped on the table by a waiter. "Honestly, been so long since I went out to dinner with anyone but friends, I don't remember. Never was much good at long-term stuff."

She loved the sound of that. He was in the same place with relationships she was in.

Maybe, if she didn't say something really stupid, there was hope for this after all.

At least short-term hope, and right now, in this new world, that was all she wanted.

CHAPTER 10

Six wonderful hours later, they both came up for air after a second passionate love-making session at her apartment.

They were in her big king bed on top of wonderful-feeling cloth sheets. The city lights around them lit up the room that she had made very much her own with a few stuffed animals a couple dressers covered with knicknacks, and cat toys.

He had fallen instantly for her two cats who seemed to think he was the best thing ever, thankfully.

Gage couldn't believe how much he enjoyed every moment with Angie, and just touching her had sent shivers through him the first time, as if making a connection he had been waiting his entire life to make.

Even though he had to be careful with some things he said during dinner and on the wonderful, hand-in-hand walk to her apartment, he hadn't enjoyed time with anyone else like that before.

She rested beside him now, trying to catch her breath, her beautiful body wonderful in the lights through the window. She didn't seem to be even in the slightest bit modest in front of him, which he also loved.

Finally, she rolled over to face him. "Where the hell did you come from?"

He laughed. "You honestly don't want to know."

She moved in to kiss him, then pulled back. "How about from this moment forward no more secrets ever from each other."

He looked deep into her wonderful eyes and then nodded. "Deal. No more secrets."

He had to do this, so he might as well start now.

"So where are you from?" she asked.

"If I'm going to tell you the truth," he said, "I first have to show you something."

"Do I have to get dressed?" she asked, smiling at him, "or is this something more intimate?"

"I think getting dressed might be a really good idea," he said, laughing and then kissing her hard. "I want to show you my place."

He loved kissing her more than he even wanted to admit to himself.

"Oh, bummer," she said. "She rolled off the bed and headed to the bathroom.

"Trust me," he said, "seeing my apartment will be worth it."

"It had better be," she said as she disappeared.

He laughed. She had no idea at all what was coming.

Ten minutes later they were both dressed and standing in the middle of her living room near the front door. The main room of her apartment was amazingly comfortable, with books scattered all over the place, a couple of nice quilts on a large chair and a tan couch, and a wall full of books.

He had never allowed himself to spy on her in this apartment, so this had been a pleasant surprise. He only followed her when she left.

He took her hand and looked into her wonderful brown eyes and smiling face. "What you are about to experience will be a shock, but please keep that brilliant mind of yours open and together we'll get through this to the other side."

She frowned. "What's in this apartment of yours?"

"A lot of books and some computer equipment, just like here, only nowhere near as nice and no cats, sadly," he said.

Then he squeezed her hand and touched his ear and said, "Two to come aboard."

"Clear."

The next moment he had transported the two of them to his apartment.

He thought her grip on his hand might break it as she looked around.

"What the hell just happened? And what are we aboard? And how?"

He could hear the panic in her voice.

"This is my apartment," he said, waving his arms around. "You asked me where I am from, this is it for the moment, but now let me answer your real question as to where I am from."

Without giving her a chance to ask a question, he jumped them both to an observatory lounge.

It was empty except for a few folding chairs. The room was large enough to hold banquets in it and one entire wall was clear and looked out over the Earth below.

He could feel her starting to get faint and he instantly helped her sit in a chair and pulled up another beside her, slightly facing her as she stared out at the planet Earth below.

Then she shook her head and looked around and then back at the fantastic view of the planet below. Then she said, "I thought it had all been a dream."

"Excuse me?" he asked.

"I was in a room like this one a number of days after the Event," she said, looking at him. "It was crowded with all of us from the surface and it smelled of death. The fine people on the ship were trying to give us help and food. They said they got us out of the way of a second electromagnetic pulse and then would put us back, but most of us would never remember. I remembered."

"Oh, my," he said. He was more stunned than he wanted to admit. He had expected she would be in panic and it would take help to calm her down.

She turned and looked at him. "So it wasn't a dream? That actually happened?"

He nodded. "It was a massive rescue operation from a thousand planets in this galaxy to save as many after the first Event as they could. From my understanding, they saved everyone who was alive from the second wave."

She nodded. "That's what they said. I remember clearly."

She went back to looking at the Earth below and they sat silently for a few minutes. He was doing his best to try to figure out the next step.

Then she turned to him and said, "You promised to tell me where you are from."

He pointed off to the right and said, "I was born four hundred and ten years ago on a planet much like the one below orbiting a sun in a small cluster galaxy that is a satellite galaxy to the Milky Way."

She blinked, then said, "I always knew I liked older men."

It took him a moment, then he laughed.

And she smiled, which was something he hadn't expected this soon.

CHAPTER 11

"So explain all this," she said, sweeping her arm around at the large banquet room with a wall that had a view to die for of Earth below. "Start by telling me what this ship is all about."

She needed some answers and she needed them quickly before she started making up stuff she didn't want to think about. And she could feel a lot of anger just boiling below the surface.

"The name of this ship is the *Home Stand*," Gage said. "From my understanding, about three-hundred-thousand people live and work on this ship."

"Wow," she said, stunned. "Bigger than most cities."

"It is huge," he said. "I've been on board for under a year and haven't even seen a tiny fraction of it."

"And what's it doing here?" she asked, trying to keep her mind focused on getting answers one at a time before she totally went crazy.

"It's one of five Seeder ships that are stationed here to try to help your planet recover from the Event. All are shielded from any kind of detection. No one in any of your forming governments knows anything about the ships here helping."

"Seeders?" she asked.

"Long story," he said. "How about we go back to my apartment and I'll get you something to drink and we can talk there."

She nodded to that and let him help her up. She loved his touch, the solid feel of his hands, and she really loved how he felt against her and how he made her laugh.

And the memory of being in a room like this one was there as well, and the kind people who had helped them all.

But she needed answers.

A lot of them.

A moment later they were in his apartment and he sat her on one side of a large couch. There was a blanket on one side, and as he said, his apartment was full of books and computers as was hers, and what looked to be a couple half-eaten dinners on an end table. Typical bachelor.

It looked like he sometimes slept on the couch facing a wide screen on one wall. She had done her share of falling asleep watching a movie as well and just not bothering to go to bed.

"I have water, fruit juice mix, and water," he said.

"Water," she said.

"Good choice."

He vanished through an archway to the back of the living area. She loved watching him walk and the way he moved. Even after this surprise, which she should have realized wasn't a surprise after this morning's rescue, she was still focused on him.

She needed to clear her mind and ask a lot of questions before this went too much farther.

A few moments later he came back carrying two glasses of water with ice.

He handed one to her and then sat on the couch, turned to face her. She took a sip and the fresh, cold water helped clear her mind a little more.

"So what are Seeders? Aliens?"

"All Seeders are humans," Gage said, smiling. "I'm human in case you were wondering."

"Thank heavens for small miracles. Alien sex would be a little kinky even for me."

He laughed, then set his glass on the small coffee table in front of the couch, pushing away a few books to find room.

"Humans on any planet always believe that they are the only race in the galaxy," Gage said. "And actually, that's true. Most galaxies are empty of any alien life of any type. So the job of the Seeders is to get a planet ready for human life and then seed human and animal life on that planet and then help the human civilization mature through all the problems."

She shook her head not really even understanding what he just said.

"Your home world below was seeded with humans and animal life by Seeders," he said.

"Evolutionary evidence?" she asked, not grasping still what he was saying.

"All planted," he said. "And then Seeders stick around to help each human culture survive all the problem periods and eventually jump into space."

"How many planets have the Seeders done this to?" she asked.

He laughed. "I would have no idea. Maybe all the possible planets in a thousand different galaxies. I don't think anyone knows, honestly, since it has been going on for so long. But the front line of the Seeders finished with the Milky Way Galaxy thirty thousand years ago and has moved on toward all the galaxies around the Andromeda Galaxy. I understand that this galaxy now holds about four hundred thousand human worlds. At least ones that have survived."

She couldn't even begin to imagine that scale.

"So have you ever met an alien?" she asked because she flat couldn't think of anything else to ask.

"There are no aliens that humans in any galaxy interact with. We just leave them alone in their own galaxies and move on."

She nodded. "So only humans?"

"Only humans," he said, smiling at her.

Then she remembered he had said he was four hundred plus years old.

"How do you live so long?" she asked.

He shrugged. "When I was recruited as a Seeder because I have some special gene, I just basically stopped aging and I don't get sick and I learned a bunch of other fun stuff like how to teleport."

"So Seeders are a giant force of babysitters," she said, "over younger or hurt societies."

"Some are," he said, nodding. "Others are on the front lines preparing planets and doing the hard work of getting human cultures started on new planets. And still others are explorers, going ahead of the front lines to explore galaxies to make sure there are no alien cultures."

"So are all humans Seeders?" she asked.

He laughed and shook his head. "Seeders are pretty rare and are only myths in most human societies. Most Seeders have already moved on before a human culture makes the jump between stars and realizes all that's out there are other humans.

And the Seeders that stay around and help cultures keep their identity secret, as I have to do when we are down in Portland. From what I understand, even the myth of there being Seeders falls away for most cultures after a few thousands of years."

She just looked into his green eyes, trying to even form another question. Then she remembered this morning.

"So why rescue me?"

"I was assigned to watch you when you left the city and protect you," he said. "My team, that consists of me and three others, are protecting four others who are considered special."

"So I'm special?" she asked, not really sure she liked the sounds of that. "Why?"

"Besides all the reasons I find you amazingly special, funny, attractive, and fantastic in bed," Gage said, "I honestly don't know. They say that you and I and the other four all have special Seeder genes."

"So I could become a Seeder and live forever and teleport around?"

Gage shrugged. "I have no idea, actually, but if you are game, I would be up for finding out. My team was never told why we were to protect certain people in Portland, but to just do it."

She shook her head. "I'm really glad you were there this morning."

"So am I," he said, reaching forward and touching her arm.

His touch felt wonderful and calmed her some.

She took another drink of water and put her glass down beside his on the coffee table. "Let's get more information. My brain is near explosion, but we might as well light the fuse. Realized I wouldn't be buying any of this if I hadn't remembered being on the ship before."

He laughed and nodded and pulled her to her feet.

He touched his ear. "Gage Teal and Angie Park to speak with Chairman Soma if possible."

He smiled at her and shrugged after a few seconds of silence.

After another moment a man's voice filled the room. "I would be honored. In my office."

Gage squeezed her hand and again they jumped to a new place.

CHAPTER 12

Gage smiled at Chairman Soma who still wore sweat pants and a tight body shirt. One thing about running a ship of a few hundred thousand people, you could do what you wanted it seemed if you kept the ship running smoothly and making a profit.

Gage introduced Angie and Soma shook her hand.

"Chairman Soma is in charge of this entire ship," Gage said. "Seeder ships run as businesses, so the Chairman is the head of the ship instead of a Captain as in a military structure."

Angie nodded and said, "I like that."

They remained standing and Soma explained. "I called for Chairman Ray to join us. He is a few galaxies away so will need to make a few jumps to join us."

Gage just blinked and glanced at Angie, who had her mouth slightly open and her eyes blank even trying to imagine that.

So far she had been amazing in the shock of suddenly finding herself in orbit. Far more amazing than he had been the first time it had happened to him.

But the idea that it would only take a minute for Chairman Ray to travel the distance between galaxies was just stunning to him. And he had been around Seeders for four hundred years.

"So how are you feeling about being on this ship?" Soma asked her.

"I was on a ship like this one once before in the rescue operation," she said. "So not as much of a shock as it would have been."

Soma nodded. "We expected as much. Has Gage given you a rough history of the Seeders?"

"He has," she said, smiling at Gage. "But I have a thousand more questions."

"If you wouldn't mind," Chairman Soma said, indicating a desk to one side of his room, "You can learn the history of the Seeders in just a few short seconds while we wait for Chairman Ray."

Angie looked at Gage and he nodded and smiled. "A quick and fast education system. Doesn't hurt."

He had used that system to pick up a lot of extra information on various things, including the entire history of the Event that hit this planet.

She stuck out her tongue at him and moved to the desk.

Chairman Soma just handed her what looked to be normal padded headphones and said, "Put these on."

She did and then on a heads-up virtual display near her he tapped in a code.

She closed her eyes and Gage just watched her. He had a hunch he would never ever get tired of just watching her as he had done over the last months.

After about forty-five seconds she sighed and removed the headphones.

She looked at Chairman Soma and then at Gage. "Amazing, just amazing."

He remembered that was exactly how he felt when he was finished with that quick lesson about the Seeders.

At that moment Chairman Ray appeared, smiling.

His long hair seemed to flow down his back and he was still dressed in a black silk shirt and slacks.

"Angie Park," he said, stepping forward. "it is an honor to meet you."

"The honor is mine," she said, bowing slightly.

There had been a little bit about Chairman Ray in the learning, if Gage remembered correctly.

Soma indicated they should all sit and Angie moved toward the couch and Gage stayed beside her. Soma and Ray sat in the chairs facing the couch over a wooden coffee table.

"I imagine this is very overwhelming," Ray said.

"It is," Angie said, "but it explains a lot about what happened after the Event when I found myself on one of these ships and also what happened today when Gage saved my life. But what I don't understand is why me and why now?"

Gage had those exact same two questions.

"Why you is simple," Ray said, smiling.

Gage was amazed how Ray just radiated control and confidence and calmness.

"You and Gage both have special Seeder genes in your bodies."

"Genes beyond the normal that it takes to be a Seeder?" Gage asked, surprised he had been included in that sentence.

"Very much so," Ray said. "And there are four more in Portland at the moment with the same gene. You six are the only ones in this entire part of this galaxy that we have found so far. And to be honest, there are fewer than six more in this entire galaxy and all of them are not in positions of knowledge and abilities that you six have."

"Not at all sure what that means," Angie said.

Gage looked at her and shrugged. He felt just as confused.

"It means we have a very special mission coming up that we need the six of you to lead," Ray said. "And that explains the 'why now' of your question. We have been preparing ships for this mission for almost a year. We are within six months of having all preparations complete. We only lack the three special teams to chair the three ships."

"Mission to where?" Gage asked.

"A very distant galaxy that has not been explored," Ray said. "I will fill you in on more details once you both have had time to think about this. But I can tell you this, you will be chairman of a very special ship. The fastest and most modern Seeder ship ever built. And over a million people will go in each ship with you."

"Each of us would have a ship?" Gage asked, feeling very confused.

"No," Ray said. "The two of you will be Chairmen of the same ship together. It is why the special gene is required."

Soma nodded and then said to Ray, "The other two teams are coming on board now."

"Let me guess," Gage said, "Benny Slade and Gina Helm are one team."

Ray nodded.

"And Carey Noack and Matt Ladel are the other two? Those are the four besides Angie my team has been protecting."

Ray again nodded.

Angie looked surprised. "I know and like all four of them. Did any of them know about this ship being here?"

She glanced at Gage who only shrugged.

Soma nodded. "Benny and Gina knew. But Carey and Matt will be having a similar reaction to yours."

"But because of the special gene, they will also remember the rescue," Ray said.

"I would suggest," Ray said, standing, "that the two of you get some rest and talk about this. And we will meet with the others and make the same offer. Then the six of you might want to get together tomorrow."

Gage glanced at Angie as they both stood.

Then Gage turned back to Ray. "Just so I am clear, could you summarize this offer one more time?"

"We have built three of the most modern and fastest Seeder ships of all time," Ray said. "We will give the two of you as a team the chairmanship of one of those ships. Your first assignment will be to travel with the other two ships to a very distant galaxy to explore and discover what is there."

"Chairmen?" Gage asked.

"Chairmen," Ray said.

Soma laughed. "Trust me, you will want to take this offer. This is a great job."

All Gage could do was nod. In four hundred years it had never occurred to him that he would ever be the chairman of his own ship.

Not once.

CHAPTER 13

Angie felt like everything since she met Gage at the restaurant has been a dream. She half expected to wake up in her bed cuddled with her two cats.

The wonderful dinner full of laughs, the fantastic sex, the promise of honesty which led her back to the spaceship she remembered after the event.

That ship hadn't been a dream, but then the offer to basically be the captain with Gage of a massive ship full of people just made her shake her head. She had a slightly different gene. She doubted that qualified her for such a task.

They promised they would talk with Chairmen Ray and Soma in the morning and he teleported them back to the large empty observation lounge overlooking Earth below. It was beautiful, with half the planet in night and the stars beyond it.

Gage put the two chairs side-by-side and they both sat down and then he took her hand and they sat there, staring out into space, just thinking.

His touch felt right in her hand and she really, really wanted to spend a lot more time with him. But working together on a vast trip together seemed a little much for someone she had only met this morning.

And the knowledge she had been given about the Seeders and their mission and how they did it in general was stunning. And logical. And massive on a scale she couldn't begin to yet imagine.

And what it took to seed a human world was flat amazing.

An advance Seeder ship would basically wipe out any lower level life on a planet deemed to be in the right orbit around the right kind of star in the right area of the galaxy. They would do that by smashing a large asteroid into the planet.

Then they would return in a few hundred years and start seeding plant and some lower level animal life. And over ten thousand years they would eventually seed a population of humans on the planet as well.

Then Seeders would watch over each planet, sometimes calling in full ships to help a civilization get to the next level. She found it interesting that all Seeder cultures became capitalistic and democracies.

Except for the Seeders themselves. They were pure capitalism, with every Seeder on every ship and on every planet drawing a wage. But Seeders themselves had no government. They basically just kept moving, doing the same thing from galaxy to galaxy and when decisions needed to be made, there seemed to be a number of elder Seeders who just made them.

It was the cause that kept Seeders moving and interested. Helping new cultures come to life on millions and millions of planets.

She glanced at Gage who seemed to just be staring off past the planet into the stars, lost in his thoughts.

"Does it worry you that we haven't known each other very long?" she asked.

He glanced at her and smiled, which made her feel instantly better for some reason. "Actually, a little. But remember I've been following you on your missions out of Portland now for six months. I know how smart and brave you are."

"And foolhardy," she said.

He laughed, which seemed to almost fill the empty ballroom with light, it sounded so perfect to her ears. "A little of that as well."

Then he seemed to think of something and shook his head. "Now I get it."

"Get what?" she asked.

He laughed again, this time to something he was thinking about.

Then he turned to her. "I've been wondering why us, the six of us? Besides the surface element that we have the right genes, why us."

"I wondered the same thing," she said. "Clearly the special gene develops in every galaxy."

"Foolhardy is the answer," he said, smiling at her and squeezing her hand.

Then he turned and faced her completely. "There is something that basic teaching program about Seeders doesn't talk about. That is that, when all the planets in a galaxy that survive expand out into space, they form this fantastic community. But from galaxy to galaxy, the human populations of a galaxy eventually just find a balance and stay in that balance."

"They stop expanding and exploring?" she asked, feeling very surprised that humans would ever do that.

"Exactly," he said. "My small galaxy has already reached that point and no one much does anything about thinking of getting to this larger galaxy so close."

"So to do a major risky mission as Chairman Ray made it sound," she said, "he needs young blood."

"And military training," Gage said, pointing a finger to himself. "Since there are no aliens and all humans eventually learn to get along from planet to planet, the Seeders have never needed much of a military force. And on most planets in my small galaxy, any military has been disbanded a thousand years before I was born."

"Now that makes more sense," she said, nodding. It really did. And the idea that Chairman Ray was looking for someone with experience in being brave and exploring made her feel a lot better. She was damn good at that.

He looked at her, smiling and shaking his head.

"What?" she asked after a moment.

"This morning you were trying to help tell people about the rebuilding going on," Gage said. "Now you are thinking of exploring space with an almost total stranger at your side."

She laughed and reached over and kissed him, which felt flat wonderful.

Then she asked, "What did you say about foolhardy?"

"Not your middle name I hope?" he said, smiling at her. "Angie Foolhardy Park just doesn't have a ring to it."

She kissed him again and then said, "I kind of like it, actually."

"After that kiss," he said, "so do I."

CHAPTER 14

He jumped them both back to her apartment on the surface and after a snack of cold chicken and an attempt to watch a movie in her book-filled living room, she fell asleep.

Once again he sat on her couch with her head on his lap, just staring at her. She was so beautiful with her long black hair and her wonderfully smooth skin, he could just watch her for hours.

At one point he noticed the movie was halfway over and he hadn't taken his gaze from her. But they both needed some sleep. They had major things to talk about tomorrow.

He eased out from under her and then picked her up in his arms, surprised at how light she felt. He wouldn't mind carrying her to bed every night.

She managed to wake up as he put her on the bed enough to mutter that she needed to use the bathroom.

He just sat there waiting for her, studying her bedroom and all the books and knickknacks in it that made it hers. When she came out of the bathroom she was naked. And the sight took his breath away.

It was like someone punched him in the gut.

She crawled into bed, then said, "Get undressed, silly. And turn off the light."

Then she gave him a sleepy smile before closing her eyes and going back to sleep.

She was clearly very comfortable with him being there with her. Just as comfortable as he was being there.

So he got undressed and joined her and the next thing he realized sun was peeking around the blinds on the window and she was laying in bed facing him and petting one of her two cats.

When she noticed he was awake, she said, "Do you think I can take my cats?"

He laughed. "You will be in charge of the entire ship. You can take anything or anyone you want."

"Will your team come along?" she asked.

"I sure hope so," he said. "But it will be up to them. I'm betting they will."

He moved over and cuddled beside her and she moved the cat to a position on top of her hip.

Touching her felt fantastic. Just the feel of her skin sent electric shocks through his body.

"What are you thinking about all this?" he asked after a moment.

"If you weren't here looking handsome beside me," she said, "I would have thought yesterday all a dream just like the first time on that ship."

"Very real," he said.

She touched his arm and said, "Yup, very real."

He stroked her side and shoulder.

"I know it's real," she said after a moment of thinking. "And honestly, I woke up thinking we should take the job."

He looked up into her wonderful dark eyes. "Even if we end up not getting along?"

"I hope that never happens," she said. "But if it does, we'll work it out I'm sure."

"I hope it never happens either," he said, kissing her. "But you know I have never been great at long-term relationships."

"That makes two of us," she said. "So we figure it out together."

She pressed into him and the cat left the bed in a hurry, and the next thirty minutes were amazing.

CHAPTER 15

Angie cooked a quick breakfast and she showered and got dressed in fresh clothes. This morning she put on a white blouse with a sports bra under it and jeans and clean tennis shoes. She put on two small pearl earrings as well.

Then he jumped them to his apartment and she sat on the couch in his living room and looked at his books on his coffee table while he showered and got ready as well.

She loved how comfortable she felt in his place. Except for the cats, it felt just like her apartment. And they even had been reading some of the same books.

When he came out of his bedroom and she glanced up, her breath again caught in her chest for a moment. He had to be the most handsome man she had ever seen. He had on jeans, a light T-shirt that didn't hide any muscles, and his short dark hair still looked damp. He smiled when he saw her and the smile reached his wonderful green eyes.

"You are just stunning," he said, coming up to her as she stood.

"I was thinking the exact same thing about you," she said. Then she kissed him long and hard.

"Start that and we'll never get out of this apartment today," he said, laughing as the kiss finally broke.

"And what would be wrong with that?" she asked, smiling at him.

"Absolutely nothing," he said. Then he kissed her back, long and equally as hard.

Finally, breathless, she pushed him away and said, "Can I take that for a promise for later?"

"For any time," he said, smiling at her.

"All right, then," she said, adjusting her clothes. "Let's go find out what this new job is really all about."

He nodded, then touched something in his ear she would have to remember to ask him about and said, "Chairman Soma, do you have a few minutes for Gage Teal and Angie Park?"

A moment later Soma's voice came back clear to Angie. "It would be an honor. In my office."

"Is this honor thing normal?" she asked Gage just before he jumped them there.

"Not in the slightest," he said.

Chairman Soma stood from behind a huge wooden desk and came around to shake both their hands.

Chairman Ray had been sitting on the couch and he stood and also shook their hands, smiling.

"I just finished speaking with the other two couples again this morning," Ray said, "and it seems they are all very interested in hearing more about the job. Have you decided to join us as well?"

Angie was surprised at that, but only slightly. She glanced up at Gage who was looking at her with those wonderful green eyes.

"Well?" she asked.

"I'm game if you are," he said.

"I am if you are," she said.

Then she turned back to Ray. "It seems we also are interested in hearing more."

"Wonderful," Ray said, smiling.

Chairman Soma seemed to be beaming like a proud grandparent watching his grandkids grow up.

"So what is the next step?" Gage asked.

"We need to give you both advanced Seeder training," Ray said. "We will need to do that on my ship. It will take about twenty minutes and another hour to answer your basic questions."

"And this training is different from what I took originally," Gage asked.

"It is," Ray said. "It will activate the special gene both of you have and answer so many questions."

Angie nodded. "At any point, Chairman. Before I get cold feet."

Gage had told her it had taken only a few minutes for him to go through the basic training and learn how to be a Seeder and understand Seeders at a base level. But she really had no idea what she was about to learn or experience, even after the short introduction program last night.

Gage laughed. "Ready as I'll ever be considering I have very little idea what this is really all about."

Ray smiled and then turned to Soma. "We will return here in just over an hour."

Soma nodded and a moment later the three of them were in a conference room with a large wooden table surrounded by leather chairs.

A beautiful woman with short black hair stood facing them.

She had on a black silk pants suit and pearls around her neck in a choke-collar fashion. Angie felt she radiated not only incredible beauty, but a depth of knowledge and age, even though she didn't look much over forty.

"This is my wife and co-chairman, Tacita," Ray said.

Gage bowed slightly and said he was honored.

Angie did the same, feeling stunned.

Tacita smiled at both of them. "The honor is mine, I assure you."

"We have one more jump to make to our ship," Ray said.

He moved over beside Tacita and as they touched, the four of them appeared at the top level of a massive room.

Angie had no sense about how far they had jumped, but she had a suspicion it was a great distance. At some point she hoped to really deeply understand the distances and even how large a galaxy really was.

A good dozen people were working around the room at stations on three levels. A huge screen filled one wall and two massive chairs sat in the lower level facing the screen. The two chairs looked like they were molded together.

This was clearly a command center of a massively large ship.

"Wow," Gage said, looking around. "Is this a mother ship?"

"It is," Ray said. He indicated they should come over to the left of the room and sit in two chairs side-by-side.

"Well," Gage said to her as they sat down. "Here we go."

"Together," she said, smiling at him.

He nodded and smiled back. "I like that part."

"So do I," she said as they both placed their hands where Ray told them to.

And around her the massive control room just vanished.

CHAPTER 16

Gage pushed back from the console when the machine released them.

He felt as if an entire library had been downloaded into his mind and sorted and stored. He knew it was there and knew he could access it all with a thought.

He was amazed he didn't have a headache.

And now he understood far more about what being a Seeder really was. He knew the entire history, everything, about them, and what fantastic work they did making sure humanity got a start in as many galaxies and on as many planets as they could.

It made him very proud of the work he had done in a small way over the last four hundred years.

He knew that, barring an accident, he would now live basically forever. He had sort of realized that before, but never given it much thought and now was not the time either. Living forever and not aging had never been a consideration for him.

He stood and helped Angie to her feet. Her eyes looked sharp, focused.

She turned with him and both of them bowed to Ray and Tacita.

Gage knew that Ray and Tacita were the first chairmen of the very first mother ship and that right now they were thirty or more galaxies away from the Milky Way Galaxy.

Gage turned to Angie. "Are you all right?"

"I am filled with awe and amazement and thankfulness and wondering why I was given this honor," she said, softly.

"We can explain it all," Ray said. "Let's go sit and talk."

A moment later the four of them were back in the comfortable meeting room where they had met Tacita. Different forms of drinks and snacks were aligned along one wall. Gage was surprised he felt hungry, but he did, so he made himself an iced tea and took a large, fresh-feeling glazed doughnut.

Angie got herself a cup of hot tea and three peanut butter cookies.

Then all four of them sat at the end of the large table and just talked.

Angie had the most questions, but she clearly knew the answers almost before she asked them. And he knew the answers the moment she did as well.

They really had been picked because of the special gene they both had been born with. And that gene allowed them many things. It allowed them to remember things and details over centuries of time. It allowed them to teleport vast distances, far more than any regular Seeder. And it allowed them to co-chair a mother ship.

Gage didn't know the mission that they were being recruited for, but he had a hunch it was because of their ability to co-chair the huge ships. Until today he had never been on a mother ship, and actually thought them a myth.

Finally, Ray returned them to Chairman Soma's office with the plan that he and Tacita and the three couples would meet for the first briefing on the coming mission in five hours.

Gage was looking forward to that.

Angie was holding Gage's hand and when they appeared in Soma's office, without Ray, Gage said, "Thank you for the use of your office for all of this."

Soma bowed deeply to them. "It has been my honor. And please, if there is anything I can do to aid you or your mission, do not hesitate."

Gage told control that two were going to the surface and jumped Angie and him back to her apartment.

She first went and found both of her cats and petted them while he sat on the couch. Then she came back and sat down beside him.

"I have to be dreaming," she said.

"The fact that I am with the most beautiful woman on the planet is a dream," he said. "Not sure what you are dreaming about."

She laughed and took his hand and leaned her head against his shoulder.

They sat like that for a few wonderful minutes, both lost in their own thoughts. Then she said, "The Seeders are amazing. How have they managed to just keep going and going for hundreds and hundreds of thousands of years?"

"Fresh recruits like us," he said and she nodded.

"Ray and Tacita want that freshness for whatever they have in mind," Angie said. "That much is clear."

"Very clear," he said. But darned if he could really figure out what the mission might be considering what he now knew about Seeders. This had to be something very new. And that excited him.

"It makes me sad that so many human civilizations just stagnate inside their own galaxy," Angie said.

"I'm not sure if having a galaxy spanning civilization could be called stagnating," Gage said, laughing. "But yes, it does seem that by taking out of most populations the Seeder gene as recruits, eventually the desire to move outward by every culture is replaced by a desire to remain solid and happy and working in other things besides exploring."

"You think the Seeder gene is what always made humans look to explore?"

"As logical as anything," he said.

"So what do we do now?" she asked.

Gage smiled. "We have hours. I am thinking a leisurely walk to one of the fine restaurants in this neighborhood, then back here for some private connection time, then off to the meeting with the others."

She pushed off his shoulder and looked at him, smiling, the smile in her eyes as well. "You think an early dinner might get you into my pants?"

"A guy can hope," Gage said, smiling back.

"Okay," she said. "I suppose I can be bought, but I'm not cheap."

He laughed. "All right, I'll spring for dessert as well."

"Deal," she said, and kissed him.

And they damn near skipped the dinner. They would have if they both hadn't been so hungry.

SECTION TWO
THE MISSION AND GETTING READY

CHAPTER 17

Angie felt excited to see the other four members of this mission. She had known and liked all four of them.

Ray had said the briefing would be in Chairman Soma's office and she and Gage had been the first to arrive.

Soma greeted them with a bow and asked what he could have brought in for them to drink. Both just asked for water.

A moment later a woman's voice in the air said, "Chairman Soma, Gina Helm and Benny Slade asking permission to come to your office."

"Please," he said, and a moment later they both appeared.

Gina was tall and lanky and looked strong, far stronger than Angie. She had dark, short hair and wore a white long-sleeved blouse with the sleeves rolled up and jeans.

Beside her Benny was as tall as Gina, but far wider and very muscled. He was ex-military and it showed in his posture and short, dark hair, cropped close. He had also been originally from

New York and had saved many lives there by setting up huge buildings as refuges after the Event.

As a couple, Benny and Gina had always intimidated Angie, but she had really come to like them over the last year since they came to Portland from New York.

Both of them smiled when they saw Angie and they both hugged her, congratulating her on joining the Seeders.

Then Angie introduced Gage.

Benny smiled. "So it's your men who have been keeping an eye on us over the last six months."

"They that obvious?" Gage asked, laughing.

"Not in the slightest," Benny said. "In fact, they are damn fine."

"Good to hear," Gage said. "I'm hoping they'll join up to come along on whatever we are going to be doing."

"That would be damn great if they would," Benny said.

At that moment Chairman Ray appeared with Carey Noack and Matt Ladel. Both were looking a little shocked and Angie didn't blame them at all. She was feeling the same way.

Carey was a tiny woman and all muscle. She had short brown hair and very light skin. She wore a blue blouse and jeans and tennis shoes. Matt was as tall as Gage or Benny at six foot, and he too was all muscle. He had short brown hair that Angie had never seen combed and large brown eyes.

Angie went and hugged them both and the others congratulated all three of them for joining the Seeders.

Angie felt so much better now that Carey and Matt were here and she wasn't the only new blood in the room. And having her there also seemed to bring Carey and Matt back into their eyes a little as well. Clearly Chairman Ray had been giving them extra help over the last few hours.

Angie felt lucky that she had Gage beside her.

After the bottles of water for everyone arrived, they all sat in Chairman Soma's couches and chairs. Only Ray remained standing and Soma went around behind his desk to watch, but be out of the picture.

At that moment Tacita appeared beside Ray and bowed a greeting to all of them.

Angie just felt in awe seeing her and her amazing beauty.

"It's time we tell you what this is all about," Ray said. "We have been planning this for about three years now, since we found all of you with your special genes during and around the rescue operation here."

Angie was sitting next to Gage in one of the big chairs and she reached over and took his hand. She noticed that Carey and Matt were also holding hands on the couch and Benny and Gina also held hands across two chairs.

Clearly Ray and Tacita had recruited three couples.

"All of you now know from your training," Ray said, "how very rare true alien advanced life is throughout the known universe."

All of them nodded.

Angie had been surprised at that more than anything else in the vast learning from this afternoon. Most galaxies had no growing or even starting alien sentient population. And Seeder scout ships spent a vast amount of time searching before any Seeder ships entered the galaxy to start seeding.

And on any galaxy that alien life was found, no matter at what level, the Seeders simply watched in secret and the seeding ships went around, leaving the entire galaxy to the alien race.

Very, very few alien races ever made it off their original planets and only two alien races had made it to other stars before falling back into ruin and then destruction. Without Seeder help, almost all human worlds seeded would face the same exact fate. Even with Seeder help, many still did.

It seemed it was very, very difficult to survive as a culture and expand into space.

And that was not counting the natural disasters that almost wiped out the human population on the planet below.

Ray went on with Tacita standing beside him saying nothing.

"Three years ago this was found in deep space heading for an edge of this galaxy," Ray said.

A hologram of what looked like a blackish pile of wadded-up junk appeared floating in the middle of the room. The pile of junk was clearly artificially constructed, but Angie could make no sense out of it at all.

"This is an alien ship," Ray said. "It is the size of a small moon, larger than even Seeder Mother Ships."

Angie was stunned, as she could imagine those that found the alien ship had to have been. Seeder Mother Ships were also the size of small moons, but shaped like a bird in flight, not like a pile of junk.

"The ship has been on trans-tunnel drive for about two hundred thousand years. The shields of the ship failed about a hundred thousand years ago. Nothing is alive on the ship."

Stunned silence filled the room as they all just stared at the hologram of the alien ship floating in the middle of the room.

Angie had a very hard time imagining two hundred thousand years. That number just seemed impossible.

"Are the alien drives designed for flight speeds between galaxies?" Gina asked.

Ray nodded. "They were. Basically just trans-tunnel drives, taking all fuel from the space it traveled through. We have been studying that ship now for the last three years. Every detail of it."

"What did the aliens look like?" Benny asked. "Were you able to tell that?"

Angie wasn't sure she wanted to know that, but was glad Benny asked.

"Short mammals with fur on their bodies," Tacita said. "Two arms with hands with six fingers on each hand. Legs used for climbing as well as grasping. A moderate brain capacity."

"They looked something like this," Ray said, "from what we have gotten out of the records on the ship and from what remains of those on that ship that were protected."

An image of a very alien creature appeared in the air. It looked like a cross between a badger and a raccoon, only with a huge head and huge and powerful shoulders and arms.

"Rats," Benny said. "They look like damn rats. I hated those things in New York."

The alien had close-set dark eyes and a long snout with sharp-looking teeth, so Angie could see where Benny from New York thought that.

"They stand about two feet tall," Tacita said. "Very powerful."

"Damn large rats," Benny said.

Ray went on. "From what we could tell from remaining records on the ship that we have been able to translate, they could have up to thirty offspring, lived between twenty and thirty of our years, and were extremely aggressive."

"So why the mess of a ship?" Benny asked.

"This is what their original ship looked like," Ray said.

Angie watched as the hologram shifted to a sleek arrow with six fins.

"As something went wrong on their mission to a nearby

galaxy," Tacita said, "and they found themselves going into deep space with no hope of finding a nearby galaxy soon, they started to build onto their ship to allow for the extra population growth."

"They managed to scoop up materials from the vacuum of space just as trans-tunnel drive takes power from the slight particles in deep space. They created this ship, along with ways of feeding the constantly growing population."

The hologram slowly morphed into the image of the ball of trash that had been there before. Only now Angie could see the ship inside the additions.

"They made it work for almost a hundred thousand years," Tacita said, "before the ship's systems collapsed from overload and their shields failed."

"At three generations every one hundred years," Gage said, "that's impressive. Three thousand generations were born and died on that ship. Wow."

Angie just stared at it, feeling a deep sadness for alien creatures that had died a very long time ago just trying to stay alive.

Even if they did look like rats.

CHAPTER 18

Gage felt stunned by all that he had heard so far. Aliens had actually developed a society that had managed to get out of a galaxy. That was both exciting and scary beyond words.

And to hear about the tragic tale of this one spaceship was amazing.

In the advanced information they had gotten earlier, he now knew what all the aliens Seeders had discovered over the years looked like. Spider-like creatures with large brains, other mammal-like creatures like these, and even some strange squid-like creatures that had actually managed to get to their nearest star systems.

"So what mission are you thinking of us doing that concerns this alien ship?" Gina asked, looking away from the ship to Ray.

Angie and Gage did the same, Angie squeezing his hand.

The hologram of the ship vanished showing a mostly two-dimensional illustration of a vast number of galaxies. The galaxies were no more than points of light and the hologram looked more like a white cloud floating there in the air.

"This is cut along the lines the alien ship traveled in two hundred thousand years of trans-tunnel flight," Ray said.

"Wow, that's a lot of distance," Benny said.

"It is," Ray said. "The small dot here is the Milky Way Galaxy and Andromeda Galaxy and other local group galaxies and all of these other dots are galaxies or clusters of galaxies the ship got near, but clearly not close enough to help them with whatever problem they were having."

Gage watched as a line appeared from the Milky Way back through all the other dots to one galaxy that must have been the start of the two hundred thousand year voyage.

"We believe the ship started here," Ray said.

The dot expanded to become an image of a group of galaxies. The line ended in the center one.

"We think the ship was trying to reach this galaxy," Tacita said, and one of the close galaxies to the main one lit up. "But something went horribly wrong and they passed the galaxy by and went onward."

"We do not know from the records we have translated so far if this was just a standard milk run, or the first exploration run to another galaxy," Ray said.

The hologram vanished.

"What we are hoping you can do with three new ships," Ray said, "is go find out what these aliens are up to and if they are expanding in this direction and so on."

"In essence," Tacita said, "a scouting mission."

Gage sat back and Angie squeezed his hand.

"I'm just a little confused," Matt said. "Are you asking us to go on a two hundred thousand year one way mission?"

Ray shook his head and smiled. "No, thanks to two brilliant inventors who actually met in orbit over this planet during the evacuation ten days after the Event, new breakthroughs have happened in trans-tunnel drive."

"The first breakthrough since humans left our original galaxy," Tacita said, "besides making the drives safer."

"So how long should this trip take?" Gina asked.

"At full speed of the new drives," Ray said, "about ten years. But we expect you will do a little exploring along the way, so a little longer."

Gage again just shook his head. He couldn't even imagine that speed and not even the training earlier today on the real scale of Seeders helped him with that.

"Two hundred thousand years down to ten?" Gina said. "How is that even possible?"

"In short," Ray said, "trans-tunnel drive opens up a tunnel through space so that a ship can travel far, far faster than the speed of light."

All of them nodded. Gage understood that as well. He even knew the math of it from his college days.

"What the two new brilliant inventors did was figure out a way to open multiple tunnels inside open trans-tunnel flights."

"Basically," Tacita said, "If you are going ten times the speed of light inside one tunnel, and then open another tunnel inside that tunnel going ten times the speed of the other tunnel, it factors to a hundred times higher. These inventors have come up with a way to open ten tunnels inside each other safely if needed."

Gage just sat there shaking his head. He and Angie were going to lead one of three ships to visit the first aliens to ever create a culture that could leave its own galaxy.

It was no wonder Ray and Tacita wanted young people who

were used to the unexpected and had lived with that being normal. There was no telling what they would run into on the other side of that ten-year journey.

And no telling what they would find along the way, either.

Damn, this was scary.

And exciting.

CHAPTER 19

Angie was starting to feel overwhelmed again. But with slow breaths, she just let her new learning from earlier kick in.

The woman who had been helping find new people to tell about Portland yesterday was at a slight war with the woman who was now a Seeder and knew all the history and details of being a Seeder.

Yesterday she thought that aliens didn't exist and humans were the only ones in the galaxy. She had been partially right about the humans being the only ones, but now she knew aliens clearly did exist.

Just an unimaginable distance away.

Across from her Carey and Matt were also looking somewhat shocked. And neither had said much at all.

It was Benny who again broke the silence in the room by asking the next obvious question, but one Angie had not thought of in the slightest.

"What kind of ships will we be using?" Benny asked.

Ray nodded and a hologram of a beautiful spaceship appeared floating in front of them. It had the look of a beautiful bird in full flight. The front was a long neck and the nose came down to what looked to almost a point.

"Three identical ships," Ray said. "Each are mother ships in size and will carry over a million people each."

Angie just opened her mouth, then shut it.

Over a million people?

Her stomach twisted into a knot.

"Each ship will have two hundred scout ships, a couple hundred seeder ships, and two hundred military ships as well," Tacita said. "All equipped and built with the new drive."

"These three new mother ships are state of the art," Ray said, "with full shields and defensive and offensive weapons capabilities, something we have never built into a mother ship before now."

All Angie could do was sit there and stare at the beautiful ship with her mouth open.

"The ship's names?" Gina asked.

"Gina, you and Benny will command the *Star Rain*," Ray said.

Angie liked that name.

"Carey and Matt, you will command the *Star Fall*."

Angie liked that name as well.

"And Angie and Gage, you will be in command of the *Star Mist*."

Angie instantly loved the name.

Matt finally spoke up. "I am not certain why you think that Carey and I can command a ship carrying more than a million people into a situation as you have described."

Beside him, Carey nodded and Angie felt herself nodding as well.

Ray and Tacita both smiled.

"The advanced training you all took to be sitting here," Ray said, "is just the tip of the knowledge. Once you have been accepted by your ships, which are sentient in their own ways, you will be given the next stage of training."

"So we will be trained?" Angie asked, feeling very relieved on hearing that."

"Completely," Tacita said. "Just the first basic part will take nine days. And you will always have your ship to help you with anything you need."

Silence for a moment as that sank in.

Then Ray went on. "Over the next six months you will be in charge of picking your crew and getting to know your ship completely. Carey and Matt, we will help you with the crew aspects of things. But as Chairmen of a Seeder mother ship, your command is your command."

"We believe you all will be perfect for this critical mission," Tacita said. "We need your youth and ability to think in any situation."

Suddenly Angie realized how Ray and Tacita were talking. This was a very, very rare position. And why Soma had bowed to them.

"Without any more hesitation," Tacita said, "we would like to introduce you to your ships. And give you the information you need to make a real decision."

Benny and Gina nodded.

Angie looked at Gage who smiled and nodded.

"Why the hell not?" Angie said.

Ray looked at Carey and Matt, who seemed to just sort of be staring at each other.

"Would you two like to meet *Star Fall?*" Ray asked.

Matt nodded first. Then Carey nodded and smiled.

"It is a beautiful name," Carey said. "So as Angie said, why the hell not?"

Ray turned to Chairman Soma. "Would you show Angie and Gage the command center of *Star Mist* and the command chair?"

Soma stood and bowed slightly. "It would be my honor."

And a moment later Angie found herself standing in a massive command center next to Gage and Chairman Soma.

"Welcome, Chairmen," a soft female voice said not only out loud, but seemingly in Angie's head. "I am *Star Mist*."

Angie suddenly felt at home.

CHAPTER 20

Gage was once again stunned at the size of a command center on a mother ship. And how comfortable he felt standing in it.

The ceilings were far overhead and the room had three levels, each about two steps higher than the one below it.

The back level was the highest and went halfway around the room, filled with stations on both the walls and facing inward. From the looks of it, a good forty people could work on this level if needed.

The next level down was also a half-circle, with all the stations facing a massive wall screen that had to be two stories tall and even wider.

On the lowest level, right in the center was what looked to be two massive, high-backed chairs that were molded together, facing the screen.

The Chairmen's chair.

His and Angie's chair.

And then *Star Mist* said in a very warm and soothing female voice, "Welcome, Chairmen. "I am *Star Mist.*"

Beside Gage, Chairman Soma bowed.

"It is an honor to meet you," Angie said, also bowing slightly.

"It is my honor as well," Gage said.

"Thank you," *Star Mist* said.

Gage looked at Angie, whose eyes were wide and she was smiling.

"Chairman Ray would like me to show you your command chair," Soma said, indicating they should go down to the lower level. "From there *Star Mist* will give you a sense of your ship."

Angie took Gage by the hand and led him down the two levels. All the stations along the way were dark, but he had a hunch he would know what each station was for very shortly.

When they stepped down onto the lower level, Chairman Soma stopped on the second level.

Clearly being on the command level was only for the two of them.

The command chair was stunning in design. One piece molded plastic with what looked to be comfortable cushions.

"The chair will form to your size and shape," *Star Mist* said.

"Thank you," Angie said.

"You are welcome," *Star Mist* said.

Gage turned to Angie. "Are you ready? Because I have a hunch when we sit down in this chair, everything will change for us."

Angie nodded. "I can't say I'm not scared out of my mind right now."

"More than facing those people in the compound the other day?" Gage asked, smiling at her.

"No, not that kind of scared," she said, laughing. "Scared of the unknown, the future, my ability to do this wonderful task that has been offered to us."

"I feel the same way," Gage said, squeezing her hand. "So let's be scared together."

"Deal," she said.

She smiled and kissed him.

And then holding hands, they sat in the big chair together, she on the left, he on the right.

Instantly the chair started to form around them and Gage felt it shape to fit his body perfectly. And it fit perfectly where he held Angie's hand.

The chair actually came out over the top of them, placing them in a sort of shell with the open side facing the huge screen as they tipped back slightly.

"Wow, this is comfortable," Angie said.

"Perfect," Gage said.

And then suddenly Gage could feel and sense Angie beside him. He couldn't read her thoughts, but he felt closer, like they were a team connected completely.

She turned and smiled at him and he smiled back.

"Like that closeness?" he asked.

"More than I want to admit," Angie said.

And Gage could sense and feel *Star Mist* as well, as if just on the edge of his thoughts.

"May I start by showing you the layout and progress of construction?" *Star Mist* asked.

"Please," Angie said.

Gage could feel her excitement and her worry, both. Somehow, *Star Mist* had linked them lightly together through the chair.

And almost instantly Gage could sense he knew the ship, where the three major ship's hangars were, how many thousands were working on *Star Mist* at this very moment and what they were doing.

It felt as if he was inside *Star Mist*, the personality of the ship, and knew her.

And knew what she knew about the ship.

And he felt he liked her at once.

"Wow," Gage said after a moment. "Very impressive."

"Thank you," *Star Mist* said. "Construction is on schedule."

"Very good to hear," Angie said.

"Now I need to take you to meet with Chairman Ray and Chairman Tacita," *Star Mist* said. "Please do not be alarmed. This will only take a moment."

The shell of the chair closed in over them, leaving them holding hands but slightly in the dark.

Gage could sense Angie's sudden worry, but he had a hunch it matched his own.

There was a slight sense of movement, then the front of the chair opened back up and it was clear to Gage they were no longer on board the ship.

Star Mist said simply, "Welcome to Earth."

Every planet humans settled was called Earth. Gage's home world was called Earth, as was Angie's. But the way *Star Mist* said it, and he was connected to *Star Mist* now in his mind, he knew, without a doubt, he was on the very first Earth.

The actual birthplace of all humanity.

And that just scared him more than he wanted to admit.

CHAPTER 21

Angie had a hunch she knew what *Star Mist* meant when she said, "Welcome to Earth" from Angie's earlier training. But she didn't want to think about that. And yet she knew because she felt connected to *Star Mist* at a very deep level.

And that connection felt comfortable and right.

In front of them was a massive circular room with two levels. They and the command chair were on the top level with nothing else around them and what looked like a plain wall that closed in the room around the top level with large pictures of stars and planets giving the wall color over the grayness.

In the center of the room, five steps down were a couple dozen couches and chair arrangements with end tables and coffee tables. A table with snacks and drinks ran along one side. All were in brown shades and a few small flowering plants separated some of the chairs and couches from others.

There looked to be a light brown carpet on the floor.

Surprisingly for the size of the large room, it felt comfortable and she could smell a light odor of baking bread.

"You may leave the chair," *Star Mist* said. "I will wait for your return."

"Thank you," Gage said before Angie could.

"You are more than welcome," *Star Mist* said.

Gage helped Angie up and they stepped out of the chair and down the five steps from the top level.

Angie still felt slightly connected to *Star Mist*, even when not sitting in the chair. That felt comforting, actually.

Then Gage pointed. "See all the rings?"

Angie could see that all the way around the top level were rings in the floor spaced evenly. The *Star Mist* command chair sat in one of the rings, the molded, high-backed chair standing proudly, but all alone at the moment.

"A meeting place for all Seeder mother ship chairmen," Angie said, softly. "Wow."

She just felt stunned. And considering how many trillions of human planets in thousands and thousands of galaxies, only having this many slots for mother ship chairmen was frightening. There couldn't be more than a hundred around the room, if that many.

After learning about the Seeders yesterday, she had wondered how the Seeders made decisions and it seemed she had just gotten her answer.

And now it looked like she and Gage were part of that very limited group.

They were in way, way over their heads.

Of that she had no doubt.

As they were about to turn toward the couches, another chair shimmered into place beside their chair and then opened up, all without a sound.

Benny and Gina sat inside, holding hands, their eyes wide.

"Welcome to Earth," Angie heard *Star Rain* say to them.

"The *first* Earth?" Gina asked.

"It will all be explained," *Star Rain* said. "I will wait here for your return."

Benny and Gina stood from the chair and saw Angie and Gage standing there. They came slowly down the five steps, looking around as they did.

"Looks like they are set up for a party," Benny said.

Then Benny looked at the top level and saw all the rings and then the two command chairs filling two of the rings.

Angie could tell he instantly understood.

Benny and Gina stood, looking around at all the rings, then Gina said, "Wow, are we in the fricking deep end of the pool."

"I feel like a kid with a pedal bike with training wheels being asked to ride a Harley," Benny said.

All three of them laughed at that. Angie was feeling the same way. All this was happening so fast.

"You all right?" Gina asked Angie.

Angie just smiled. "I am so far past my comfort zone, I can't remember what it felt like. So thanks to Gage here, I'm just going forward."

Gage laughed and said, "If you think all this is just a daily happening for me, we need to talk."

She laughed and squeezed his hand. "Who knows what lurks in a guy's past."

"Not this," Gage said, waving his arm at the large room, "I can assure you."

At that moment another chair shimmered into place beside the other two and opened up to show Carey and Matt sitting, holding hands, eyes wide as well.

They both looked to be on the verge of complete panic.

"The children are all here," Benny said. "Now where the hell are Mom and Dad?"

CHAPTER 22

The six of them finally moved down to the couches and food. All of them took a bottle of water and a few cookies, just talking about how out of place they all felt.

And way over their heads.

Having all of them feeling the same way seemed to help Matt and Carey and Angie a little, but Gage couldn't even imagine what they were feeling right now. His transition into a Seeder had been fast, but over a six-month period where he had managed to get used to spaceships and flashing around in space and helping human cultures and so on.

These three were only on their second day and in a position where someone was telling them they were going to be responsible for a million people. He didn't feel even close to ready for that. And he was over four hundred years old.

He was the oldest of them all by far, actually, since Gina had been a Seeder for just over a hundred years and Benny for less than four years. So he couldn't imagine how they were all feeling if he felt completely overwhelmed.

Finally, after about ten minutes, another chair shimmered into place almost on the opposite side of the large room and it opened to show Ray and Tacita.

They were holding hands and Ray helped her up from the chair and the two of them walked hand-in-hand to the group. The two of them still clearly loved and respected and cared for each other.

And the rumors were that they were hundreds of thousands of years old.

Gage sure hoped that he and Angie could be still feeling that way in ten years, let alone in thousands of years. Considering both of their problems with relationships in the past, that was going to be a question.

Right now he would just take tomorrow with her, he felt that lucky.

Tacita had them all sit on couches together, one couple per couch. Then she and Ray took chairs facing them.

"So is this really the original Earth?" Gina asked.

"It is," Tacita said, nodding. "You will learn the complete history of mankind over the next few days as you go through the training."

"Nothing whitewashed or left out," Ray said. "It was a bumpy path to where we find ourselves now."

"No other way with humans," Benny said.

"So true," Ray said, smiling.

"How many Seeder mother ships are there?" Gage asked.

"At the moment, counting your three, twenty-seven. But others are built and in transit empty to various galaxies, and others are in construction as well."

"We need many more, "Tacita said. "That's why bringing three more mother ships into active duty is such a special event."

Gage was surprised there were so few. Very surprised.

"And we were picked to be the chairmen of the three new ships because of our special genes?" Angie asked.

"Yes," Ray said, "partially. But you were mostly picked for your youth. You will understand far more after your training."

"So what exactly is to happen next?" Benny asked.

Gage had been about to ask that same question.

"You have nine days in a row of extensive training here," Tacita said. "We will return after each session to eat with you and answer questions anyone has. Between sessions you can go back to your homes and rest and talk."

"This first session will not only give you a history of all of humanity," Ray said, "but trigger your advanced genes to allow you to be in better contact with your ships."

"All three of your ships are very pleased with each of you," Tacita said. "They will become your friend, your constant companion, and be there for anything you need."

Gage squeezed Angie's hand and she smiled at him. In the background he could still feel *Star Mist* with him. And he liked that feeling.

"They will help us get past this feeling of being totally inadequate?" Matt asked.

"They will help, yes," Ray said, smiling. "And the teaching coming up will help as well. We would not put you in charge of a Seeder mother ship for such an important mission if we did not believe you could handle the task. And the ships would have also rejected you if they felt that you were not up for the job."

Matt nodded.

Gage also nodded.

Ray and Tacita stood.

"Now take your partner's hand," Ray said, even though all three couples were holding hands already.

"And relax," Tacita said.

As Ray and Tacita turned to move away, an opaque bubble formed around each couple and then snapped down tight over them.

Gage could feel a massive amount of information flowing to him.

He could also feel Angie beside him and through her hand.

And together they went down into the flow of knowledge.

CHAPTER 23

The next nine days seemed to go by instantly to Angie, yet they took forever at the same time.

The first session had lasted three hours and she felt like her head might explode with the vast amount of information. But at the same time, she felt calmer and also she could sense *Star Mist* was with her.

And she could also sense Gage. It felt like she was no longer alone and she loved that feeling.

After every learning session each day, Ray and Tacita joined the six of them for dinner in the large room to answer questions.

As each day went by, Angie felt more in control, more sure that she and Gage could do what they have been asked to do.

And it was clear that the other two teams felt the same way.

By the time the teaching was over, and they were having their last dinner together in the main room, questions had turned to the coming mission and the final construction of the three ships. And how to pick and recruit the crew for not only each mother ship, but for all of the smaller ships on board.

After each day during the learning period, Angie and Gage had gone back to her apartment in Portland. They had taken a nap in each other's arms, then walked down to the first restaurant they had eaten at and had a quiet dinner, not really talking about anything, but just being together and letting the information soak in.

Then each night they had gone back to her apartment and made love. And with each day, she had felt more and more connected and in love with Gage at such a deep level, she couldn't believe that level had even existed.

So on the afternoon before the last day of learning, they had decided to jump to the chairmen's living quarters on *Star Mist*.

The huge apartment had taken Angie's breath away. It wasn't furnished, but it had four bedrooms. Two for beds and two for offices. It had a huge living room with a stone fireplace. There was a kitchen and dining area that was a dream, with every modern appliance she could imagine and a few she didn't know the function of as well.

She had felt instantly at home, even though there wasn't a stick of furniture in it.

Instantly.

They had wandered through the huge place, hand-in-hand, including standing in the two monster walk-in closets that were larger than her bedroom back in Portland.

And the apartment had a bathroom off of each walk-in closet and another major bathroom near the fantastic living room.

"We've known each other for just under two weeks," Gage had said as they stopped on the edge of the living room and he took her in his arms. "You ready to move in with me?"

"Pretty fast there, lieutenant," she had said, smiling up and him and then kissing him.

Then she had eased back and looked at the man she had completely fallen in love with and that she felt she now knew better than any person she had ever met.

"On one condition," she had said.

He smiled and had said, "Name it."

"That we only have one huge bed in this place, so we can always sleep together."

He had laughed. "Deal."

Now, as all eight of them sat having a wonderful dinner turkey and dressings and some side dishes after the last learning session, the mood was excited and even Carey and Matt were feeling completely confident.

Angie loved the food. After the learning sessions, she always felt so hungry. And she flat couldn't believe her mind had been able to grasp everything that had gone into it. Yet it had.

"I have one question that seems to be nagging in the background," Benny said.

"Fire away," Ray said.

"There seems to be a fear of this alien race," Benny asked. "Is that because human cultures become so passive over time?"

"Exactly why," Tacita said. "There are entire galaxy-spanning human civilizations that have existed for hundreds of thousands of years that have no military ships or even would think that way. Most human cultures would have no way to resist an aggressive alien culture if attacked. Too many centuries of breeding that nature out."

"Again why the youthful leadership of this mission," Matt said. "Makes sense."

Angie nodded to that. It made complete sense now.

"So why do Seeders have no historical memory?" Gina asked. "Why are entire galaxies just left on their own to have the fact that they were seeded fall into myth and legend?"

"Human nature," Ray said, shrugging. "When there is no threat, humans don't care about where they came from, what is on the other side of the same galaxy, or even on the other side of their own planet."

That was so true Angie didn't want to think about it.

"We tried to maintain a cultural memory for the first few hundred galaxies we helped start with human life," Tacita said. "But it never held and no one seemed to care and we eventually dropped the idea."

"Do all the chairmen meet at one point or another?" Gage asked.

Angie realized that wasn't in the information they had been fed either.

"They do," Ray said. "Every year. We meet here and have dinner and talk about the future and how everyone's projects are progressing. Next meeting is in about two hundred days. We will let you all know ahead of time, I promise."

"We do it on the anniversary of the launch of the first mother ship to seed another galaxy," Tacita said.

"When was that?" Angie asked, again wondering why that information wasn't in the rest of what they had learned.

"About six million years ago," Ray said.

"Wow," Angie said and the others seemed just as impressed.

Seeders had been moving from galaxy to galaxy for over six million years. How had she become so lucky as to get to be a part of all this?

"Whose ship was that?" Benny asked, taking a second helping of the fantastic smelling turkey.

"It was our ship," Ray said, smiling at Tacita.

Tacita nodded. "We took it out and I can remember the fear like it was yesterday."

Ray gently rubbed Tacita's shoulder with affection before both of them went back to eating.

Angie and everyone else at the table just stared at Ray and Tacita.

And it took a moment before anyone else took a bite of anything.

CHAPTER 24

Over the next six months after training, it surprised Gage of how much needed to be done. And the five who lived in Portland had to come up with reasons for leaving the city for an extended period of time so that no one would notice that they had vanished.

Angie had moved her two cats into their apartment on *Star Mist* and the two cats took to it without a problem, clearly enjoying the extra room to run and not seeming to miss the lack of windows.

Angie and Gage had spent one day furnishing the apartment and stocking the kitchen with dishes and everything else they would need.

Gage loved living with Angie every day as well, and it felt at times they could almost read each other's minds. Not quite, but they clearly knew what each other was thinking most of the time.

And every time they sat in their command chairs, that feeling grew stronger.

They spent a vast amount of time for the first two months overseeing the last of the construction and learning every detail of the moon-sized ship. They knew it from their training, but both of them wanted to see everything firsthand as well, from the storerooms to the hanger decks.

And *Star Mist* helped them make sure they didn't miss a detail.

Gage really loved being so close to *Star Mist* as well.

And Angie had learned quickly how to teleport, which had been a fun day of practice and excitement.

For the next four months, they also worked on putting together a bridge crew. Actually they needed three shifts of a bridge crew, the main shift and second shift and third shift.

Both Angie and Gage agreed that Gage's second-in-command, Drake, should be on the bridge in the main bridge crew and in charge of the entire military side of things for the ship.

Ray and Tacita agreed, so when Angie and Gage explained the mission and offered Drake the job, with the original team helping him in various positions, Drake just damn near lost it.

After he pulled himself together, he had said simply, "Hell yes."

But their best find was their second-in-command of the entire ship, which they put into place five months before launch. They had asked Ray if Chairman Soma would be insulted at the offer and Ray had just laughed. "I doubt it, but you would have to ask him."

So they had talked to Soma and offered him the second-in-command position if *Star Mist* approved him and Soma had said yes instantly.

And *Star Mist* had loved him.

So with Soma working with them and all of his knowledge of

what was needed in a bridge crew, the first main bridge crew formed within two months.

And then each bridge crew member suggested others on down below them, and a second shift and third shift bridge crew took shape.

By the time the entire bridge crew was staffed, there was still two months until launch, so they had lots of time to run drills and make sure everything on board was ready. And both Angie and Gage liked everyone on all three shifts on the bridge.

Even though many of the crew members were far older than even Gage, they showed Angie and Gage immense respect. Often more than both wanted.

Gage very much appreciated that.

All three ships' crews came together at about the same pace.

And what Gage found amazing was that the bridge crews of each ship were from fifteen to twenty different galaxies in this area. And many had had hundreds of years at positions with other bridge crews. But it seemed, to be on a bridge crew of a Seeder mother ship that was to be sent on a very special mission was a real honor.

Not one person turned down the offer.

Almost from the first week after the learning sessions, the six chairmen had made it a habit to meet once a week for dinner in one of the chairman's apartments to talk and plan.

And laugh.

They did a lot of laughing.

Often Ray or Tacita or both would join those dinners.

Those dinners had helped them all get closer. And by the time the week before launch, they knew each other and trusted each other completely.

Gage could not have imagined a better group to take such a risky mission with.

All of them knew the path they would be taking to the target galaxy and had studied it, but what they did along the way had been a matter of discussion.

That was finally settled out during the last dinner before launch.

Gage and Benny as military men had put the plan together and presented it to everyone including Ray and Tacita after a yummy meal of fresh fish and salad prepared by Angie and Matt.

They were in Angie and Gage's apartment, sitting around the large wooden dining table. It was mostly square and Ray and Tacita sat at the end of the table with their backs to the wall, Angie and Gage sat with their backs to the kitchen, Benny and Gina with their backs to the living room, and Carey and Matt with their backs to the bedrooms.

"Here's Gage and my suggestion for a plan," Benny said. "All three mother ships would head out at near top speed past the range that Seeder scout ships have already explored."

Gage was stunned at how far they were going to go outside of Seeder areas. The distance already explored was less than one percent of the total distance they planned to travel.

"Then in all galaxies near the intended path after that," Benny said, "all three mother ships will stand off the outer edge of the galaxy and launch one-hundred-and-fifty of the two-hundred scout ships to do fast scans of the galaxy looking for alien life and also looking for any signs of the aliens that we are headed toward."

"A military ship will go with each scout ship," Gage said, "for protection and also to help with the scans."

"So the three mother ships would pause near a galaxy," Ray

said, "then launch nine hundred ships total to cover the galaxy, leaving one hundred ships in reserve in each mother ship. Correct?"

"Exactly," Benny said.

Gage nodded and went on. "Since all the scout ships and military ships are equipped with the new trans-tunnel drive, the surveys of an entire Milky Way-sized galaxy should take around a week from what we have figured out after talking to experienced survey ship chairmen."

"They wouldn't do as deep a survey as scout ships normally do that takes decades to complete," Benny said, "but they would make sure no aliens existed at any level in the galaxy."

"And if there are aliens?" Angie asked.

"If we find an alien race at a lower level," Gage said, smiling at her, "we go ahead and still survey the entire galaxy and then move on. If we find a more advanced race, then we stand off and take data, but not do a full survey."

"Very good thinking on that," Tacita said, nodding.

"As we have discussed," Benny said, "every bit of data would be returned to the home base now being constructed on the edge of the Milky Way galaxy to track and monitor the mission."

"But by doing it this way, taking our time to get to the target, we get a lot of data collected along the route of the alien ship."

"How many galaxies are you talking about doing a fast survey of?" Ray asked.

"Seven hundred and ninety galaxies of various sizes before reaching the target galaxy," Benny said, "so the trip to target should take around sixteen years, counting the time in transit between galaxies."

Gage was very happy to see everyone around the table nodding at the idea.

"Would all the ships reload back on board the mother ships after each stop?" Gina asked.

Gage glanced at Benny.

"If the distance between galaxies is close, no," Benny said. "But on the longer distances, yes."

Gage took a deep breath and went with the next idea he and Benny had. Neither liked it much, but they could see no choice.

"We also want to send ten scout ships and ten military ships from each mother ship ahead to the next galaxy," Gage said.

"Even with the arms and shield on these three wonderful mother ships," Benny said, "we don't want to drop into the middle of an advanced and armed civilization."

Silence filled the dining area. Gage flat hated this idea, but no military person wanted to go into a possible combat area without knowing what they were walking into. So he completely agreed with Benny.

Finally Ray nodded. "That makes sense."

"A suggestion," Tacita said.

Everyone turned to look at her.

"The scout ships hold upwards of thirty thousand lives, including crew families. Correct?"

Everyone nodded.

"And the military ships we have built hold around twenty thousand crew and family," Tacita said.

"That's right," Benny said.

Ray nodded, clearly understanding where Tacita was going.

"What would be the bare minimum crew that each ship could function with completely?"

Again silence.

"I honestly never asked that question," Benny said.

Gage hadn't either, but he liked where this was going.

"So are you suggesting," Carey asked, "that the ten scout and ten military ships from each ship set up residences for their crew's families on board the mother ships?"

"Not permanent homes," Tacita said. "Rotate a different ten scout and military ships each time to scout ahead, so each family would only be displaced for a few days every six months or so."

Gage glanced at Benny who was smiling.

"We both hated this idea," Gage said, "because of the great risk of life. This will hold the risk to reasonable levels and we are not asking spouses and children to be in harm's way."

"All know the risks of this mission," Ray said.

"But managing the risks this way for many is a good plan," Gina said.

"I agree," Angie said. "And I like the overall plan of taking our time getting to the target."

"Agreed," Ray said.

"Agreed," Tacita said.

"Then we have a plan," Benny said, smiling.

Gage was smiling as well.

It was time to get moving. And that had him excited, more than he wanted to admit, considering they might be flying into a mess.

A mess that might cost the over a million people on each mother ship their lives.

SECTION THREE
THE JOURNEY

CHAPTER 25

(THIRTEEN YEARS LATER)

The call came in from the scout ships working ahead on the 614th galaxy that they had found a problem.

Angie had been working on dinner and Gage was in the command center, making sure everything was in good order with the most recent galaxy survey before he came back to their apartment for the evening.

They tended to work all the time, often in their own offices, checking every detail of everything on board the ship. During the day they had made it a habit to get out to either the military area or the scout area to talk with people.

Those on board liked the fact that the chairmen had made themselves open to talk with. It didn't reduce the respect, but actually increased it.

The thirteen years since launch had gone smoothly in all the surveys so far. Out of the six hundred plus galaxies they had surveyed, two had sentient alien life at planetary levels. One was a race of large ant-like creatures with massive heads. The second one was a form of ape-like creatures, very different from humans, but clearly working to build a civilization.

The three ships had quickly surveyed the galaxy and moved on.

"Angie, to Command," Gage said, his voice almost echoing through their apartment. In thirteen years, that had never happened.

She wiped off her hands, took off her apron, and jumped to his side in the command center.

"We have a problem up ahead," he said, taking her hand as they sat down in their command chair.

The familiar feel of the chair wrapped them and the heads-up display appeared.

"We are here," Gage said.

"We are linked in as well," Benny said.

"Standing by," Carey said.

Angie was stunned. They had all practiced linking the ships a few times, but nothing had come up that needed it until now.

"Go ahead, Chairman LeAnne," Gage said.

Chairman LeAnne's face filled the screen for a moment and *Star Mist* fed Angie the fact that she was the chairman of *Blue Bay*, the lead scout ship exploring the next galaxy ahead.

Chairman LeAnne was thin, with very short brown hair and a deep frown on her face.

"We have found a dead galaxy," LeAnne said. "We have only been here and taking preliminary readings from the edge, but something really nasty tore an advanced civilization that had thrived here apart."

"You're going to need to explain more, Chairman," Benny said.

"From our initial scans the moment we dropped out of trans-tunnel drive," Chairman LeAnne said, "we thought we were facing an advanced, galaxy-spanning civilization. All signs were in place, from orbiting stations around thousands of planets. So we all remained completely shielded and made sure no scans could be traced. All our ships spread out around the outer edge of the galaxy to get a clear picture of what was happening."

Angie knew that was all standard procedure.

"Here are some of the scenes we found," Chairman LeAnne said.

An image of a former large city smashed to nothing. Blackness and ruins. There wasn't even any plant life.

Another quick series of images appeared, all about the same showing total destruction.

"All of these images were taken on planets scattered around the galaxy," Chairman LeAnne said.

"What kind of power could do this?" Carey asked softly, not really as a question, but saying out loud what all of them were thinking.

Looking at the ruins, Angie knew the signs of what she was seeing from what had happened back home.

"This didn't happen that long ago," Angie said.

"You are right," Benny said.

"About fifty standard years ago," Chairman LeAnne said, "from our initial scans. And pretty much to all planets at about the same general time."

"Any idea what this race looked like?" Matt asked.

Chairman LeAnne nodded and then said softly, "They were from our target race."

Angie felt her stomach cramp down into a knot that she had a hunch wouldn't clear for some time to come.

CHAPTER 26

For the next three hours, Gage and Angie studied all the information coming in, not leaving their command chair. And staying in touch with the other two ships as well.

They called back all ships from their current galaxy and all ships were back on board the mother ships within two hours. Then all three mother ships headed toward the dead galaxy at full trans-tunnel speed.

The scouts, working from the edge of the dead galaxy, discovered what had happened on each planet. Some sort of weapon had basically ignited the entire atmosphere, sending a massive wave of fire and intense winds over every foot of the surface, burning it all and knocking everything into piles of rubble.

Even if one of the aliens had survived that, they died instantly because all oxygen was completely burnt away from the atmosphere.

The scouts also discovered that there were over six-hundred-thousand planets destroyed, all with cities on them. No planet without a colony or a city on it was touched, which eliminated the chance this was some sort of natural disaster.

And every ship in space and every space station was destroyed in the same way.

Every member of the entire alien race had been wiped clean from this galaxy.

Stunning carnage, just stunning. Gage couldn't even begin to wrap his mind around it.

Just about the time Gage was feeling exhausted and famished, Chairman LeAnne asked to be linked to all of them once again.

The three mother ships were still three hours away from the dead galaxy.

When the link to all three mother ships was up, Chairman LeAnne put up a hologram of the galaxy. It was a standard spiral galaxy about half the size of the Milky Way.

"The destruction started here," Chairman LeAnne said, having a red color appear on one edge of the galaxy.

As Gage and everyone watched, the red spread through the galaxy.

"How long did that take?" Gina asked.

"Six weeks approximately," Chairman LeAnne said.

Gage knew exactly why it took that long. It had taken him twelve weeks to get from one side of the Milky Way Galaxy to Angie's home planet in standard trans-tunnel flight. This galaxy was about half the distance across.

"That's the speed it would take at standard trans-tunnel flight," Gage said to everyone else.

"Damn, good spot," Benny said. "*Star Rain*, could you tell us how many ships would it take to do that, stopping at each planet along the way for less than one hour standard?"

"Four hundred and twelve ships," *Star Rain* said.

"I concur," *Star Mist* said to just Angie and Gage.

"*Star Mist*," Gage said, "assuming the killing fleet left the galaxy approximately at where they finished their attack, what would be their possible next galaxy targets? Please show us all."

"And how long would each possible target take for them to reach at standard trans-tunnel speed?" Angie asked.

"I have illustrated the answer with a sphere to show the farthest distance standard trans-tunnel flight would allow a ship to go from the edge of the destroyed galaxy," *Star Mist* said.

A shimmering three-dimensional image appeared in front of Gage and Angie.

Gage's stomach twisted when he saw there were galaxies inside the sphere.

"How many galaxies are inside that range?" Benny asked.

"Seventeen," *Star Mist* said to all the chairmen.

"Thank you," Angie said, her voice soft.

Gage could tell she felt as worried and upset as he did. Something very, very ugly was happening ahead of them.

"Thank you, Chairman LeAnne," Benny said. "Please continue your research. We will have more help for you shortly."

She nodded and vanished from the link.

"I suggest we all rest and link back up in two hours before we reach our destination," Carey said.

"I agree," Gina said.

"Two hours," Gage said.

Gage stood and helped Angie out of the chair. The next instant he had teleported both of them to their apartment.

They needed the time to think.

This kind of situation was the very reason Ray and Tacita had picked them.

Now it was time to find out if Ray and Tacita had made the right decision.

CHAPTER 27

Angie felt much better after a light dinner and time to just sit quietly with Gage and think while sipping on after-dinner coffee in front of their fireplace.

She couldn't believe that they were an hour away from a galaxy where just six months before an entire civilization had been wiped out.

She couldn't grasp that amount of death and she sure couldn't grasp any reason for it.

She turned to face Gage. His strong, handsome face looked a little rested and not as haunted as he had looked earlier. And he seemed ready to get back to work.

"The way I see it," she said, "we have some sort of major war going on."

He nodded. "Either between two factions of the same race or two different alien races."

"So what are we going to do either way?" she asked.

"We keep researching what happened exactly while at the

same time we find out where the fleet of ships is located," Gage said.

She nodded to that. That was what she had been thinking as well. "But then what? Do we stop the destruction by siding with one side or the other?"

He shook his head. "We cross that bridge when we come to it. But humans have never taken a non-interference stand since the mess in our first galaxy. I don't see this being any different."

"Except we don't interfere with any alien cultures," Angie said. "These are alien cultures."

"We have walked into a mess," Gage said, laughing and shaking his head. "Let's see what the other chairmen are thinking."

Angie and Gage put their coffee cups back on the kitchen counter and jumped to the command center. The main bridge crew was still at their stations and second crew was backing them all up, sometimes with two people working at the same station together. Giving each other breaks and double-checking everything was a standard procedure in these kinds of emergencies.

But this was the first time Angie had seen it in operation outside of a drill.

They dropped into their chair and *Star Mist* caught them up to speed quickly on the reports that had come in.

The other four chairmen had just connected in as well when Chairman LeAnne again signaled she had an update. At this point the three big ships were just over an hour away.

"We found the remains of an attacking ship," Chairman LeAnne said.

"Details and on screen," Benny said.

In front of Angie appeared an image of a sleek, swept-back winged ship that seemed to shimmer against the blackness of space. The ship looked like it could easily go through atmosphere. And it had a fairly close resemblance to a Seeder ship.

The sight of it took Angie's breath away.

"How large is that ship?" Gage asked.

"The size of a normal scout ship with room for about seventy thousand to live," Chairman LeAnne said.

"Survivors?" Carey asked.

"We are too far away to tell," Chairman LeAnne said.

"Thank you, Chairman," Benny said. "We will be in touch within the next hour, but keep us apprised of any more developments."

Chairman LeAnne nodded and the link broke.

"So who has any ideas?" Matt asked.

Between the six of them they went over what Angie and Gage had discussed.

All of them agreed with sending scout ships after the fleet. But now that they had found a ship that had been a part of the fleet, they all agreed that a few more hours would make little difference. They would first investigate that ship and what it was capable of doing.

They agreed a normal-sized group of scout and military ships would continue on forward to the next galaxy in their plans to see what was there.

And that a group of thirty scout ships and thirty armed warships would spread out in groups of ten pairs going after the fleet to see where it was.

That left most of the scout ships and military ships to go over this dead galaxy with a fine scan, to make sure nothing was missed.

Then it was Gina who asked the question that Angie hadn't thought of.

"Do we bring Ray and Tacita in on all this, beyond sending back all the information we have gathered?"

"Can they get here?" Angie asked. She knew that relay stations were being built out from the Milky Way along their route, and she knew that Ray and Tacita could teleport across vast distances.

"They can get here," *Star Mist* said to everyone.

"How fast?" Angie asked.

"Within an hour," *Star Mist* said.

"I say they need to be here," Benny said.

"I agree," Gina said.

Carey and Matt both agreed and so did Gage.

"*Star Mist*," Angie said, "Would you please invite Chairmen Ray and Tacita to an emergency meeting in one hour in our chairmen conference room? Please have drinks and light snacks available for everyone. Inform us all when they have arrived."

"I will do so," *Star Mist* said.

"Thank you," Angie said.

And then for the next hour the six of them went over every detail they knew so far and the three mother ships took up positions in various places around the edge of the dead galaxy.

The next wave of scout ships was sent onward toward the next galaxy and five scout ships surrounded by ten military ships jumped to the location of the invading fleet damaged ship.

Reports would be flowing in soon and they would have a lot more knowledge.

"Chairman Ray and Chairman Tacita have arrived in the conference room," *Star Mist* said.

Angie nodded and somehow felt slightly relieved as she and Gage stood and jumped to them.

CHAPTER 28

Gage nodded to both Ray and Tacita as he and Angie appeared and then took their seats near the head of the table. It was their ship, that was their positions.

Ray wore his normal silk shirt and dark pants that seemed to make his long silver hair shine. Tacita wore a dark silk pants suit that seemed to glisten as she walked.

Gage hadn't seen them since launch thirteen years before, but they hadn't changed in the slightest, which didn't surprise him considering their vast age.

Ray and Tacita took seats at the end of the table and a moment later Carey and Matt appeared and sat down on the left side with a nod to Ray and Tacita. And then Benny and Gina did the same, sitting on the right.

"I am assuming," Angie said, starting off the meeting, "that you have not heard of our discovery yet?"

"We have not," Ray said.

"*Star Mist*," Gage said, "please bring up a hologram of one of the destroyed planets."

City rubble as far as the eye could see and then the hologram pulled back to show the destruction was on a massive scale.

Gage watched as both Ray and Tacita looked shocked.

"Our scouting teams found this on every formerly inhabited planet in this galaxy," Benny said. "Basically the oxygen in the atmosphere was ignited causing a massive fire storm that swept around the globe and destroyed the world."

"The aliens who lived there were the aliens we came in search of," Matt said.

That snapped the heads around of both Ray and Tacita to stare at Matt.

"Bring up an image of the galaxy, please, *Star Mist*," Gage said. Gage knew that Ray and Tacita were not going to like this at all.

The ruins vanished to show the small spiral galaxy floating in the middle of the table.

"Please run how the destruction pattern went through every planet with these aliens on it," Gage said.

The red spread from one side of the galaxy to the other.

"Every planet with a civilization on it in the entire galaxy was destroyed in six weeks, the time it took a ship to travel through the galaxy at standard trans-tunnel speed," Benny said.

Ray and Tacita looked completely shocked.

Gage remembered a few hours before that he felt the same way. In fact, after watching that again, he felt shocked once more.

"It would take a fleet of at least four-hundred-and-twelve attacking ships to do this," Gina said.

"And this all happened six months ago," Angie said.

Gage didn't know what Ray and Tacita were thinking, but their faces had gone cold and hard and actually angry.

"*Star Mist*," Gage said, "please bring up the illustration of how far the attacking fleet could have flown since this attack."

The image of the sphere appeared in the air over the conference table.

"We plan to send out three teams of ten scout ships and ten military ships," Benny said, "to find the fleet. And we have our standard ten scout ships and ten military ships already on the way ahead to our next scheduled galaxy to see what they will find there."

Ray nodded.

"But we have not sent the scout ships after the fleet yet because we found remains of an attacking ship," Matt said.

"*Star Mist*, please show us the image of the attacking ship."

The sleek, shining, winged craft appeared, glowing against the darkness of space.

Ray gasped and Tacita said, "Not possible."

And at that, all six other chairmen turned to look at them.

And if Gage didn't know the two humans sitting across from him were millions of years old, he would have sworn both of them were going to be sick like children.

CHAPTER 29

"Would you mind filling us in on what you are thinking?" Angie asked, staring at the pale faces of Ray and Tacita. They both looked like they had gone into instant shock.

Ray nodded. "You have scout ships moving toward that ship?"

"Scout and military ships are at the ship now," Benny said.

Ray looked at Angie and Gage. "May I have permission to ask *Star Mist* a few questions?"

"Certainly," Angie said and beside her Gage nodded.

"*Star Mist*, would you illustrate with a dot the original galaxy of humanity and the galaxies around it, all on the same scale? Mark the original galaxy by having it blinking."

"Be glad to, Chairman," *Star Mist* said.

A hologram appeared above the table far enough in the air that everyone could still see each other under it without a problem.

The hologram looked to be a vast field of thousands and thousands of stars and clusters of stars, but Angie knew each point was a galaxy with billions of stars. The scale that Seeders worked and thought at still surprised her, even with the training and the last years of being on board this wonderful ship.

"Would you pinpoint this galaxy on the star field you are showing?" Ray asked.

The scale got smaller slightly and more thousands of points were added until one point of light blinked. It looked like a vast white cloud was hanging over the conference table.

"*Star Mist,* would you show the positions of all of these galaxies three point five million years ago," Ray asked, "adjusting for galactic drift and then draw a line between the two blinking points?"

The dots of light shifted slightly and a line appeared.

"Please now make the Milky Way Galaxy on this chart blink and draw a line from the original galaxy to it as well."

Another line appeared, only shorter. But Angie could see that the two lines formed what looked like a slice of pie out of all the galaxies. And they had just traveled along the crust of the pie to get here.

"*Star Mist,* at standard trans-tunnel drive," Ray asked, "how long would it take for a ship to travel from the original galaxy to this galaxy?"

"One-point-four million years," *Star Mist* said. "Without stopping."

"Oh, shit," Tacita said and put her head down on the table.

Ray just sat back and stared at the image of galaxies floating over the table.

Angie and the rest of the new chairmen just sat silently.

A few moments later, Tacita sat up straight and took a deep breath. Then she said, "I have no doubt that you will find that attacking ship to be of human origin."

Angie kind of had a hunch that was where all of this was heading, but it still surprised her.

"Why would humans wipe out an entire galaxy full of sentient creatures?"

Tacita opened her mouth to say something, but Ray touched her arm and she just shook her head and closed her mouth.

"We're out here risking our necks," Benny said. "And the lives of millions of others. I think we deserve to know what you were about to say."

"They believe they can kill these creatures because they created them," Ray said.

Tacita nodded. "I was not going to put it that nicely."

Angie just sort of stared at both of them. "They create an entire race of intelligent creatures and then destroy them. Why?"

"Why in the early days of all human civilizations do humans use animals to experiment on and then put them down?" Ray asked, anger clearly not far below the surface.

"But this was a galaxy-wide civilization," Carey said.

"Just a different scale of experiment," Tacita said, almost spitting her words.

Angie felt sick to her stomach. She didn't want to believe that civilized humans were capable of such things. This went against everything the Seeders knew and believed.

"This is disgusting," Benny said.

"They think we are just as disgusting," Ray said.

Angie finally couldn't take it any longer. "Are we going to get to know what happened all those millions of years ago and how you know all this?"

"And why we didn't learn it with the basic briefings?" Gage said.

"We didn't include it because we didn't think it was possible," Tacita said.

"And it happened almost a half million years after the origin of the original galaxy," Ray said, "after we were already Seeding and expanding outward though many galaxies."

"What was possible?" Carey asked a moment before Angie could.

"We never thought it possible that a fleet of ships could survive over a million year trip through space," Ray said.

Angie looked at the shining ship on the screen, floating dead in space. Clearly they had survived just fine.

CHAPTER 30

Gage was feeling more annoyed than anything else.

He and Angie and over a million people on this ship had all come out here to risk their lives trying to find out about another galaxy-spanning race and suddenly they learn about some fight between human factions millions of years ago.

Not happy was the least of how he was feeling right now.

And Gage could tell that Benny and Gina and the others were also slowly building to anger.

Gage had a hunch you did not want to see the six of them really mad at anything.

The room was deathly silent and the star field hung high over the table like a bad cloud.

"I would say," Benny said, "that you owe us a story and a real explanation of what the hell is going on."

"Agreed," Matt said.

Gage just nodded, almost afraid to say anything.

Ray and Tacita both nodded.

Gage was sure they could feel the anger building as well. None of the six of them were covering it very well.

And beside Gage, he could feel Angie almost vibrating.

"I can assure you," Ray said, "that it did not dawn on us in any fashion that this alien race might be human created until just now. And we may still be wrong about that conclusion."

"We are not," Tacita said.

Benny held up his hand and stopped them both. "The beginning. Start at the damn beginning, would you?"

Ray nodded, took a deep breath and started into the story. "About a half million years after we first launched our ship to start Seeding other galaxies, we found a new alien race."

"The ants?" Gina asked.

Gage remembered that from their training.

"The ants," Ray said, nodding.

"We chose at that point to develop the policy," Tacita said, "of leaving alien races alone completely, letting them develop or not develop at their own pace."

"But that policy was very, very controversial," Ray said, "because without intervention and help from Seeders, no human-seeded planet would survive through the many steps that destroy a civilization. We learned that with hard lessons."

Gage nodded to that. He knew from the training that the fact that humans survived at all was by sheer luck through numbers of major periods and setbacks along the way. Most alien civilizations the Seeders had found had not.

"So intervention is a way of life for Seeders and we are proud of the work we do," Tacita said.

"But many thought that the same policy should extend to alien races," Ray said. "Many did not."

"Also," Tacita said, "a very strong faction had always been against the terraforming of planets we did as the first step of Seeding. The faction argued that by smashing an asteroid into a planet to clear it off before Seeding new plants and animals, we were possibly destroying an alien life form that might evolve into an intelligent species in a million years or more."

"By simply settling on a planet, they also argued," Ray said, "even without the terraforming, human settlements and civilization on a planet would stunt and destroy any alien life chance at evolving."

Gage could see both points.

"But the data of observations of billions of planets inside the life zone of yellow stars showed that was not going to be the case," Tacita said.

"In fact," Ray said, "before even the first attempt at terraforming happened, the studies had covered just under nine billion earth-like planets in many galaxies, many of the planets very, very old in their life cycles. No higher level life had evolved or emerged."

"We find evolved life now on about one planet in sixty galaxies," Tacita said. "Do the math on that. And none of the alien civilizations we have found evolved to a civilization that could span outside their own galaxy. And only two spread into their own galaxy at all before destroying themselves."

"So there was a division in ideas," Benny said.

Gage was glad Benny was trying to keep this on track.

"A very strong one," Ray said, nodding. "The other side believed in two things we Seeders do not believe in. They believed in helping an alien race evolve when found and they also believed even more in the genetic building of an alien race from life forms found on a planet."

"Seriously?" Gina asked.

"Holy shit," Benny said.

Ray nodded and went on. "They experimented in a galaxy far too close to the home galaxy. They built a race that eventually tried to take them over."

"The fight was short and very quick," Tacita said.

Ray nodded again. "Seeder military ships came in and saved the remains of the human population in the galaxy from the race they had created."

"Let me guess," Benny said, "you destroyed the experiment."

"We did," Ray said, nodding. "We had no choice, for our own safety. The race they had created was a very aggressive conquering-type race that did not believe in letting any other race live, including those who created them."

"Seeders outlawed any form of that kind of experimenting into the future," Tacita said. "It's why Seeders have a firm policy of going around any galaxy with alien life and standing off and just watching and not interfering."

"And why we are out here now," Carey said, "to learn and watch and make sure this race is not a threat to our Seeded galaxies."

"Exactly," Ray said.

"So what happened next was that even though mostly destroyed, those who believed in helping alien races evolve were still vocal," Tacita said.

"So we helped them build a massive mother ship called *New Life* with hundreds of smaller ships on board," Ray said.

Gage was shocked. "You helped them?"

Ray nodded, his eyes down.

"The agreement was that the crew, just under a half-million

people who wanted to take the journey, went into stasis for one million years," Tacita said. "And after that they agreed they would continue on to get as far away from human galaxies as they could as they searched for alien races to help."

"And to build their own?" Carey asked softly.

"I'm afraid so," Tacita said.

"*Star Mist*," Ray said, "Using the same star field floating above us, would you please show from the historical records the direction the *New Life* took when it left the original galaxy."

Gage watched as on the star field hologram a red line appeared. It was not on the track of the line directly from this galaxy back to the original human galaxy. In fact, it went off almost thirty degrees to one side and ten degrees higher.

"Could you show the end of the line where the crew would have come out of stasis after one million years?" Tacita asked.

The line shortened slightly.

"Draw a line from that point to this galaxy please, *Star Mist*," Ray said.

A blue line appeared.

"How long at full standard trans-tunnel drive would it have taken *New Life* to make that journey?"

"One million, two-hundred-thousand years," *Star Mist* said.

Gage did the quick math for himself. One million years in stasis, one-point-two in travel meant there was well over a million years missing. Damn.

"So they have been exploring along that route for just over a million years," Ray said.

Gage could finally see why this had caught Ray and Tacita by surprise.

"That makes sense now," Benny said, nodding.

He was clearly not as angry as he had been and Gage could feel his anger draining away.

Much better, because now they all had to face the question of what to do next.

SECTION FOUR
THE GROWING PROBLEM

CHAPTER 31

Angie had been so angry that through all of Ray and Tacita's explanation, she had been afraid to say anything or ask a question. She couldn't trust herself to be civil.

But when the original path of the *New Life* was shown, it cleared up to her why Ray and Tacita would not have even thought to mention that part of Seeder history.

Neither of them thought it would apply to this situation.

But now what?

The eight in the conference room were sitting, all thinking, when Angie got a signal from Soma, their second in command. He knew they were not to be disturbed unless urgent, so she clicked it and said, "Yes, Soma. All the chairmen can hear you."

"The scout ships have reached the next galaxy in our original path," Soma said. "The galaxy has been destroyed as well in the same fashion, about six months ahead of this one."

"No signs of life at all?" Angie asked, her stomach twisting.

"None," Soma said.

"Hold a moment," Angie said.

Angie glanced at Gage and then around at the other four chairmen. "I suggest we send the scout ships farther ahead along our intended course."

All five of the other chairmen nodded. Angie did not give Ray and Tacita a vote.

"Soma," Angie said, "please tell the scout and military ships to move on to the next galaxy at top speed."

"I will do so," Soma said.

He clicked off and Angie looked at the others around the conference table. "Seems our distant cousins," she said, "are not only wiping out a civilization that fills an entire galaxy, but one that fills many galaxies."

"We need a lot more information as to what is happening here," Gina said.

"Angie agreed. "For example, how long did it take this race to cover this entire galaxy?"

Gage leaned forward. "Has any information been withheld from us about the ship that started all this and what we learned about this race from that ship?"

"I do not think so," Tacita said, shaking her head.

"They are a race that breeds quickly, is very aggressive, and has little if any arts or music or writing," Ray said.

"Their function was to breed and expand," Tacita said, "which was why they kept adding onto their ship until it finally could not handle any more and failed them."

"They knew that would be the outcome, but they could not stop breeding and adding on new shelter on the ship," Ray said.

Angie shook her head at that. That was deep breeding. They might have survived if they could have controlled that.

"And you saw no evidence of human tampering at all in their records?" Carey asked.

"Nothing," Tacita said.

"Nothing," Ray said. "But now that we are facing this, we will have the scientists go back and look at everything again with that in mind."

Silence, hard, nasty and uncomfortable silence.

Finally it was Benny who got to the heart of what they were all thinking.

"So do we interfere and stop them or do we stand off and watch?" Benny asked.

Once again there was silence that just seemed to cut at Angie.

"We do not have enough information to act in either direction," Gina said.

Angie nodded to that, as did Gage.

"So we send our scouts and military as planned to find the fleet," Benny said. "Shielded so they cannot be seen."

The other five chairmen nodded.

Again none of them looked at Ray and Tacita.

"And we drag every bit of information and history out of their wrecked ship," Matt said.

Again all of them nodded.

"And we find out if they really did create this alien race and how fast they spread," Gage said.

Again, the other five chairmen nodded.

Angie then turned to look directly at Ray and Tacita. "It would be our honor to have you stay aboard and observe and help us with historical questions. If you would?"

Both Ray and Tacita nodded.

"If you would allow us," Ray said, "we would be glad to put together a historical lesson of the time we described. It would only take a few minutes for each of you to be up to speed on everything about this branch of humanity."

Everyone nodded.

"Thank you," Gage said. "That would be very helpful."

Benny stood. "Let's go find some answers."

With that, he and Gina vanished.

A moment later with a nod to Ray and Tacita, Carey and Matt also vanished.

Ray looked at Angie and Gage. "We are sorry this possibility did not get discussed and shared."

"We understand," Gage said.

"Yes, we do," Angie said. "But realize you put the six of us in charge of the well-being of millions of people on these ships. We take that responsibility very seriously. That is why we were all so angry at not being completely informed as to what we might be going into."

"We understand," Tacita said.

"Good," Gage said. "So please, in prepping this new historical data, don't leave off any part of humanity that splintered off, or any major lost ships, or anything that might be what is going on here, if that really is a human fleet."

"Let all of us be the judge of what might be important or not," Angie said. "It might be the difference between saving millions or not."

Ray and Tacita nodded and with that Angie and Gage jumped back to their command center.

And for Angie, it felt good to be away from Ray and Tacita. She was still that angry.

CHAPTER 32

Gage and Angie spent two hours going over every bit of information coming in, then took a break for a quick bite of lunch, then right back to the command center.

Gage couldn't remember a time before where he had been so focused on one task.

It was at just under three hours after the meeting with Ray and Tacita that the first information started to flow in about the fleet ship.

It was a human ship.

Gage shook his head. Well, that settled that much, but was there another part of humanity that might be out here instead of the ones Ray and Tacita thought were here? That was still to be determined.

The human ship hadn't been attacked, but had engine failure and all occupants had been saved to other ships. The ship was left clearly to be salvaged later.

All systems were still up and running, but no crew were left on board.

The ship had no real weapons compared to the military ships on board *Star Mist*. And the ship only had standard trans-tunnel drives that looked very outdated.

The six chairmen were linked by their ships and had a discussion on what to do next.

"We need the data and historical information from that ship's computer," Carey said.

Gage agreed as did everyone.

"But we can't leave a trace that we were there just in case we decide to stay out of this mess," Gina said.

"Damn straight," Benny said.

Gage agreed with that, so while they were still linked, they talked to Chairman LeAnne about the possibility of downloading that ship's basic computer on board the ship and not leaving a trace.

"Easily," she said. "We can set up a perimeter to give us warning if one of their ships are headed back and we can have all that data from that main computer system in less than an hour."

"Keep it isolated from your main computers," Angie said. "Extreme isolation. No telling what traps are on there."

"Understood," Chairman LeAnne said and clicked off.

At that moment Chairman Ray contacted them all. "We may have come up with yet another possibility for that fleet being human. And we have the historical data ready to let you all have it quickly."

"We take in the history first," Gage said. "Then we will better understand this new possibility."

Everyone agreed and for the next fifteen minutes, all six chairmen, sitting in their command chairs, absorbed a detailed history of the Seeders after the first millions of years in the original galaxy.

Gage was surprised about the fifty million years after the original galaxy was settled and calmed and the first mother ship was launched. Human history had clearly not gone smoothly.

And there were many small sects of humans who had taken off into space, and one full ship of prisoners that had been exiled in the last days of the final settling of the original galaxy.

Gage was fairly convinced these humans here were not from the exiled prisoners because that ship had been sent in almost the opposite direction. The distance between where it ended up and this location would be impossible to cover even in four million years at standard trans-tunnel drive speeds.

New trans-tunnel speeds could cover it in a few hundred years, but so far there were no signs that this human group had the new trans-tunnel drive.

So which of the many fleeing sects of humanity could this one be?

After they were all finished with the history lesson, it was Matt who suggested they postpone the meeting with Ray and Tacita until they had the preliminary information from the ship.

Everyone agree and Ray and Tacita also agreed, saying that would give them even more time to dig into the types of engines and Seeder ship styles each sect originally left with.

Then, before they signed off, Angie asked the question she and Gage had talked about for only a few minutes.

"Chairmen Ray and Tacita," Angie said, "Could any of the settled galaxies along the way, say two million years ago, moved on into drive speeds that would allow them to leave their galaxy?"

"They almost uniformly do not," Tacita said.

"Almost uniformly?" Benny asked.

Silence.

Then Ray said, "We will do what we can to find out that information as well."

The conference ended.

A few minutes later, as Angie and Gage were going over what they had just learned, Soma reported to them that the scout ships headed to the next galaxy on their original route had found another completely destroyed galaxy.

Gage just couldn't believe the amount of life, alien or human, that had been lost.

"How much farther to our target galaxy from that galaxy," Angie asked *Star Mist*.

"There are forty more galaxies along the original route," *Star Mist* said.

Gage took a deep breath and squeezed Angie's hand. Then he asked, "*Star Mist*, please link us to the other chairmen again and show us an image of the galaxies surrounding our target galaxy. With the outside edge of the sphere being the galaxy we are now."

The other four came on as the image appeared in front of all of them.

It looked like a ball of bright lights.

"How many galaxies is that?" Benny asked.

"One hundred and seventy thousand," *Star Mist* said.

All Gage could do was stare at that and wonder if this alien culture had spread over all of them, part of them, or even farther.

And how they would even learn that information.

Nobody said a word.

CHAPTER 33

Angie had agreed that they should just send the small group of ten scout ships and ten military ships onward toward their target galaxy, reporting in as they got to each galaxy close along the intended path.

They needed to know how widespread this was.

More information kept pouring in from the damaged fleet ship. It had no shields that could make it invisible as all Seeders ships had standard. It was an old ship as well and had very little fire-power in weapons.

There had been a stockpile of large bombs used to ignite an atmosphere, but the bombs had been taken with the survivors.

When Angie had asked how old the ship was, the answer was not certain, but maybe fifty thousand years, if not more.

Growing up on a young planet where it seemed inventions and jumps forward in science were every day, Angie found it difficult to imagine how little humanity changed over very, very long stretches of time. At some point, when this was over, she would have to ask historians about that.

And why.

Star Mist broke into her thoughts. "The fleet responsible for the destruction has been found."

A moment later all six of them were again linked as the information came in. The location of the fleet, not very far from this galaxy, actually, was shown on a holo-image.

Data scrolled under the hologram. Seven hundred and six ships, with two large mother ships smaller than *Star Mist*, but yet still large. Large enough to carry a half-million people and even more ships.

Large enough to have a factory on board to build more ships as they went.

Angie did not much like that thought at all.

All were clearly human ships and all the smaller ships were designed in the exact same style as the ship left behind.

They were all moving at standard trans-tunnel speeds and were within three weeks of a new galaxy.

All six of the chairmen agreed instantly to have a couple scout ships with military escorts jump ahead to see what was ahead of the fleet.

Suddenly Angie had a worry. "*Star Mist*, from the data so far, did the aliens of this galaxy have a way to warn a neighboring galaxy what was happening?"

"No way of knowing for certain," *Star Mist* said.

"So a ship at full trans-tunnel speed," Benny said, "would only be a few weeks ahead of the fleet. Not much of a warning to mount a defense against what this fleet does."

A few minutes later the scout ships sent ahead reported a full galaxy of teeming alien life, the same aliens that had been in the ship found near the Milky Way.

"We have three weeks," Gina said softly.

No one else said a word.

All Angie could do was stare at the images of planets teeming with life the scout ships were sending back.

An entire galaxy of life.

Seeders prided themselves in building civilizations and saving lives. Could the three-plus million Seeders on this mission just stand off and watch an entire galaxy be wiped out.

Did they even have a choice?

What the hell were the six chairmen going to do?

CHAPTER 34

Two hours later, the six chairmen were back in the conference room with Ray and Tacita.

Gage hated that they were put in this spot, with an impossible decision. They were going to have to stop a fleet of human ships to save a galaxy of aliens.

But either way, it was now clear they were going to have to jump into the middle of something they did not want to be a part of.

Over the last two hours, the scout ships moving ahead had found another destroyed galaxy. And the data from the fleet's ship left behind had given them the last four hundred and ten years of their trip but not much more in who they were overall.

It seemed that in those four hundred plus years, they had wiped out over nine hundred galaxies full of the aliens.

And they had mapped out where there were even more galaxies full of these aliens that would take them another two hundred years.

It seemed that what had been learned from the derelict ship about the aliens was very true. They were low-level intelligence, had somehow managed to get and be able to replicate trans-tunnel ships, and they could spread over an entire galaxy of planets, adapting to local conditions in under six hundred years.

That was stunningly fast.

With the help of *Star Mist*, Ray and Tacita had a short presentation about the history of the aliens.

"They started here," Ray said. He had *Star Mist* pinpoint a galaxy on a hologram that floated above the table in a red dot. "They spread like this in just under a half million years."

Gage watched as a red tide swarmed out of the one galaxy, mostly moving in one direction.

"We have no information as to the chance they also spread in other directions," Ray said.

"*Star Mist*," Gage said, "please pinpoint the galaxy we are at now."

A white light blinked on one of the galaxies near the edge of expansion.

"The ratio on that is that every one galaxy they settled spawned at least three more," Ray said.

"A form of exponential growth," Matt said, softly.

"Shit," Benny said.

Angie just sucked in her breath and Gage couldn't believe what he was seeing.

"They must move on," Tacita said, "because they not only are constantly having over thirty offspring in a very short lifetime, but they use up each planet's resources very, very quickly by constructing buildings and millions of ships."

"Most die left behind on planets that are overcrowded and

without resources," Ray said. "Basically, every planet the aliens settle becomes exactly like the ship we found."

"Overused and dead," Tacita said.

"This galaxy the fleet wiped out was in the final stages of life," Ray said. "It had been drained of all resources by the aliens, all ships that could be built had been built and were on to other galaxies, and the hundreds of billions of aliens on these planets had already turned on each other for food."

Silence.

"They were eating each other?" Benny asked.

Ray nodded.

Intense silence in the conference room.

Gage couldn't think of a damn thing to say after that.

CHAPTER 35

Angie sat with everyone in silence for a moment. She always said that Seeders worked at a grand scale, but basically putting down an entire galaxy, like putting down a sick dog, was not at all what she was thinking.

She looked at the hologram floating above the table. The red was like a giant stain of blood covering it.

Then she had a horrid thought.

"*Star Mist,*" Angie said, breaking the silence. "Could you run a simulation of the expansion of this alien race, left unchecked over the next million years? And please mark on the scale humanities home galaxy and the Milky Way Galaxy."

The hologram shifted to what looked like a fine cloud of dots in the air over the table with the Milky Way blinking and humanity's home galaxy blinking.

"I will run this in one hundred thousand year increments," *Star Mist* said.

The red started as a small stain in one area of the dust field. It stopped and Star Mist said simply, "First Segment."

The next image had the red creeping out into a far larger red stain among the white points of light that indicated entire galaxies.

The third had the stain taking up a large area.

It was at the sixth expansion that the red stain covered the Milky Way and the seventh expansion covered the historical home for all of humanity.

"That's enough, *Star Mist*," Angie said. "Thank you."

She felt sick and once again there was silence in the room.

This time it was Benny who broke the silence. "*Star Mist*, would you bring the scale back down to the current area of the alien infestation and then overlay what we know of which galaxies the fleet has destroyed?"

The hologram again changed. The alien galaxies were represented in red, the fleet-destroyed galaxies were represented in green.

Angie saw the pattern at once. The fleet was trying to cut off the leading edge, leaving the galaxies in the center to just collapse on themselves. The fleet was trying to slow down the expansion.

And they were losing.

They were losing big time, actually.

"Shit, just shit," Benny said.

Not a person in the room could disagree with that statement.

Finally, as Angie sat staring at the images where the aliens were expanding, Gage said, "We still need a lot more information here."

"Agreed," Gina said and Angie nodded.

"Do you know who those humans are in that fleet?"

"We think we do," Tacita said, nodding. "And we were slightly wrong about our previous assumption. This fleet is not the humans who broke from the Seeders because they wanted to create alien creatures."

"Then who are they?" Benny asked.

"They call themselves The Exterminators," Ray said. "*Star Mist*, please show the timeline I gave you for The Exterminators."

The hologram of the galaxies faded and a timeline came up floating in the air.

"The fight between the Seeders," Ray said, "which Tacita and I led, and those who wanted to help alien races, and even create them, ended just about a half million years after we left our galaxy with the first mother ship."

"Because they had created a nasty race we had to destroy, all laws changed against them. We allowed those who called themselves The Creators to take the ship out a million years as we told you," Tacita said.

"But that decision was not a popular one either," Ray said.

"To say the least," Tacita said. "A man by the name of Chairman Wanderson put together a fleet that would follow the first ship and clean up after them and their mistakes. He felt it was the only way to save humanity and over a million people signed up to go with him. They called themselves The Exterminators."

"That fleet is The Exterminators," Ray said. "Or part of them or what is left of them after all this time."

Angie tried to grasp what she had just heard. "Are you saying that maybe this alien race that will sweep over our known universe was built by a group called The Creators?"

"We don't know for sure," Tacita said.

Ray shook his head. "Considering this alien race does not have the mental ability to invent trans-tunnel flight, let alone slow their own reproduction so they don't eat each other, it seems likely. This race should have destroyed itself on its home planet in the normal evolution of their species."

"So this other group is trying to clean up the mess from the first group?" Benny said.

"Seems very, very likely," Ray said.

"I would say it's about damn time we talk to both groups," Benny said.

Angie wasn't so certain about that.

And honestly, she had no real desire to talk with a group that could create an alien race as an experiment or one who could wipe out galaxies full of an alien race.

CHAPTER 36

The meeting broke as all eight chairmen went to get more information. Angie and Gage had spent the next two hours in their command chair and not a one of the two shifts of the command crew had left other than to take a short break or get some food.

Thirty scout ships and thirty military ships surrounded and shadowed the fleet, carefully trying to tap into any data they could without raising alarms or letting anyone know they were there.

Every bit of information had been captured from the fleet's ship and from that it was learned that Ray and Tacita were right. This was one of The Exterminator ships. And The Creators were not far beyond the galaxy the mission had been aiming at originally.

At one point the two groups had joined forces to stop the expansion, even though for centuries before, they had had running pitched battles. But it seemed that by the time some sanity had taken hold in the two groups, it was too late.

Now both groups were just fighting a losing battle as the race one group had created swallowed one galaxy after another faster than they could be stopped.

The Creators had given their creation the ability to build an exact pattern ship with trans-tunnel drive. Basically a transport ship. The desire to build the ship and expand into space had ended up being part of the alien driving needs, just like eating and creating offspring.

And the aliens built the ships by the millions on any planet they reached, using all resources of the planet, then jamming the ships full and sending the ships off into space to find new planets or galaxies.

It was why the aliens on the ship they found nearing the Milky Way had been unable to fix their ship. They were smart enough, barely, to build with a pattern, not smart enough to fix the ship when it broke down.

Gage couldn't get the image of this rat-like race overwhelming the Milky Way galaxy like a tidal wave swelling up over a flat beach. Humans would be defenseless at such an onslaught of sheer mass of numbers.

It seemed very clear to him now that this mission was going to be a humanity rescue mission and a mission of death to swarming masses of rat-like aliens.

He flat didn't see a choice.

They all decided they needed some rest before they made the next decision.

He and Angie had gone back to their apartment. They had both worked to fix a small, light meal, then they took a shower together and crawled into bed.

Gage woke about three hours later and Angie was already wide awake beside him.

"What are you thinking about?" he asked, moving to put his arm over her to hold her while she stared at the ceiling.

Even under this kind of extreme stress and on very little sleep, she was still the most beautiful woman he could ever imagine.

"We have to show every member of the crew of every ship," she said, "everything we know, including the outcome of these aliens being left unchecked."

He hadn't thought about that at all, but he agreed.

"We have been carrying a few hundred Seeding ships and crews," she said. "If we decide to help with stopping this alien culture from expanding, we need to let everyone who has problems with that decision head back home on a Seeding ship."

He understood exactly what she was saying. No one should be forced to help destroy galaxies full of aliens.

"I agree," he said. "But we might find another way."

"I love you for your optimism," she said, turning to kiss him.

After a moment of holding each other, something that gave him strength, he said, "Ready to go back to work?"

"No," she said. "But it seems a million or more people and the fate of all humanity says we should."

He laughed and watched her as she rolled out of bed and headed for the bathroom.

It was going to be a damn long day. He knew that, but together, they would get through it.

Somehow.

CHAPTER 37

Gage and Angie spent two hours letting *Star Mist* catch them up on all the new data coming in about the fleet, about the original creators of this race, and about the fight to stop the expansion.

As they had clearly realized yesterday, the Exterminators and the fleet of Creator ships were fighting a losing battle. They had started too late and they just couldn't move fast enough to keep up with the expansion.

And they didn't have enough ships.

Nothing had changed. Angie had so hoped it would have.

After the two hours, all eight chairmen met again in the *Star Mist* conference room and made sure all data were clear between all of them.

Then Angie suggested her idea that if the decision was to help in this fight, anyone who didn't want to remain should be allowed to board a Seeding vessel and return home.

Everyone agreed to that, but once again Gage said, "There has to be another way."

"Any way," Gina said.

"*Star Mist*," Gage said, "would you please show the edge of expansion of the alien race?"

The image came up showing the expansion and how the two other fleets were trying to stop it by wiping out galaxies, but clearly the galaxy they had just destroyed would have destroyed itself given time.

Suddenly Angie had an idea.

"If we stop the expansion," Angie said, "this race will collapse on itself and die. Correct?"

Everyone nodded and beside her Gage looked puzzled. "What are you thinking?"

"*Star Mist*," Angie said, "please show the direction in arrows of the expansion from each galaxy that is still able to produce ships."

"Of course," Benny said as the arrows appeared. "We don't destroy the galaxy home worlds, we just stop their ships."

"The alien built ships have no defenses, do they?" Matt asked.

"None," Gage said. "They are just transports."

Angie was starting to get excited. She stared at the hologram of the galaxies around them.

"I can only extrapolate from the inexact data we have at the moment," *Star Mist* said.

"We understand," Angie said. "Please try."

The arrows appeared coming from the leading edge galaxies and also the secondary edge galaxy. Behind that, the older occupied galaxies seemed to have no arrows.

"We are talking about millions and millions of alien ships in transit at any given time," Carey said. "And we can't miss one ship or this all starts over again."

Matt nodded, then said, "Possibly. But we may have the time and the speed to get ahead of all this."

"Maybe," Gina said.

"*Star Mist*," Gage said, "from the information you have at the moment, could you give us an approximation of numbers of alien ships leaving galaxies over the next six months."

"I would need a lot more data," *Star Mist* said, "but with the data I have and the number of alien galaxies we know of, in six months over sixty million alien ships will leave the alien galaxies. That number, will, of course, increase rapidly if the ships reach their destinations and build more ships."

Angie didn't want to think about that number. Not until she had more information.

"*Star Mist*," Gage said, would you estimate the average transit time of an alien ship to a new galaxy?"

"Two years on average," *Star Mist* said. "These numbers are simply estimates from the best data, you understand.

"Yes, we understand," Gage said. "Thank you."

Angie looked directly at Ray and Tacita. "How many armed ships could we get here from human galaxies willing to help in this fight and how fast could we have them here?"

"We would have to convert ships to the new drive," Ray said, clearly thinking. "Then it would take nine to ten years at full new drive."

"Ten thousand ships would be a conservative number within twelve years and thousands more per year after that," Tacita said.

Ray nodded agreement.

Angie looked around. All of the chairmen were in deep thought.

"*Star Mist,*" Angie said, "how many fighter ships are in The Exterminator and The Creator fleets combined?"

"Two thousand and ten confirmed," *Star Mist* said. "All with only standard trans-tunnel drive."

"*Star Mist,* how many ships do we have on board the three mother ships," Angie asked, "that are armed and capable of destroying an alien ship?"

"Nineteen hundred and sixty," *Star Mist* said.

Angie nodded.

"How many small fighting ships could the three mother ships build," Bennie asked, "and at what pace?"

"Combined," *Star Mist* said, "the three mother ships are capable of building two military fighters a week each."

"Could that be increased if other resources were given to the task?" Gina asked. "And the fighters made much smaller?"

"Yes," *Star Mist* said. "If the fighters were small craft only capable of carrying ten crew members, each mother ship could produce upwards of twenty per week."

Angie could feel the excitement growing around the room.

"So if we stop the ships from leaving a galaxy," Benny said, "we then don't have to worry about the aliens left teeming in the galaxy. They will follow their own natural course of events."

"Exactly," Angie said. "We contain each galaxy and stay back and don't interfere, just as Seeders are supposed to do with alien galaxies."

Ray and Tacita were nodding in agreement.

"Damn," Benny said. "We need to find out if this will work because I am not at all up for destroying billions of lives and entire galaxies full of beings."

All of them agreed to that.

"So we meet in three hours," Angie said. "Dig in, find every detail we can and meet back here. Let's figure out ways to make this plan work."

All seven other chairmen nodded and a moment later she and Gage were back in their command chair letting *Star Mist* flow data at them as fast as possible.

CHAPTER 38

Gage waited with Angie in the conference room three hours later. Both of them were munching on sandwiches and Ray and Tacita were also eating at the other end of the table.

None of them spoke, mostly because there was nothing to say until all eight were in the room. Small talk just seemed way out of place at this point in time.

But Gage was feeling good about the chances Angie's idea might work.

They had come up with a couple of details that needed to be worked out to make this entire plan even have a chance of working because it was something Carey had said that haunted Gage's mind.

We can't miss a ship or all this starts over.

So he and Angie planned on bringing up some refinements that needed to be invented and invented quickly for this task at hand.

A few minutes later the other four arrived and all four went to a side table to take a sandwich and a bottle of water. None of them had even taken a few extra minutes to eat in the last three hours.

"Okay," Angie said, addressing the chairmen, "can we do this?"

"*Star Rain* believes our window of having this succeed is closing quickly," Gina said.

Gage nodded, as did everyone else. With this sort of exponential growth pattern, there was a point of no return that even faster ships and more ships would not be able to stop. And if that occurred, Gage had decided that the fallback plan was to set up a line of defense between the aliens and the human galaxies.

He doubted that would stop the flood for long, but it was better than having no secondary plan. But he had no intention of mentioning that plan to anyone at the moment.

"I see a few major problems," Benny said. "We will be unable in short order to staff the smaller fighters."

"We have a solution for that," Ray said. "Tacita and I can jump fighter crews from the Milky Way Galaxy here when that time comes."

"Perfect," Benny said, nodding.

"Thank you," Angie said.

Ray nodded.

Gage looked at Carey and said, "You said something earlier that scares me to death."

Carey nodded. "Can't miss a ship."

"Exactly," Gage said. "So we need scientists to develop a new scanning system that is long range and can pick up any alien ship signature."

"Extreme long range," Benny said, nodding.

"We can get the two inventors of the new trans-tunnel drive working on it at once back home," Tacita said.

"And many other scientists over thousands of planets as well," Ray said.

"And all the qualified scientists on all three ships need to go after that as well," Gage said. "That detail is critical."

"So do we have any sort of plan?" Matt asked.

"I do," Benny said after a moment. "Military thinking. *Star Mist*, would you show an image of the galaxies of the aliens, extrapolating from our current best information?"

Gage saw a light dome of galaxies. It was far more than he wanted to think about.

"This image is of the possible and likely alien galaxies in this area," *Star Mist* said. "If the alien expansion is moving in other directions, that information is not available."

Silence for a moment as everyone took in that detail. But Gage felt they had to focus on what they knew at the moment.

"*Star Mist*," Benny said, "please show a green area between unoccupied galaxies and the alien occupied galaxies."

The image expanded and a green dome appeared inside the arching mist of points of lights.

"First line of defense is along that green area," Benny said. "We try to stop every alien ship we can crossing into that green area."

"*Star Mist*," Angie said, "how many alien ships does it take to settle a galaxy?"

"One," *Star Mist* said.

Silence in the room again.

Gage just felt stunned.

"*Star Mist*, how long would that one ship take to populate the entire galaxy? Ray asked.

"One ship will take approximately ten thousand years to fill a Milky Way sized galaxy."

Everyone around the table nodded slowly.

"That green line is our first line of defense," Benny said. "We slow them down."

Gage stared at the simple illustration that showed them how impossible this task was considering how much space that green dome covered.

"We won't get them all," Benny said, "so our second line of defense is scout ships that are monitoring all the galaxies in this area for any sign of construction. If we can, we stop them before they start filling a galaxy and building more ships. If we can't, we isolate that galaxy and don't let any ship out."

Again more nodding.

Gage could see that this would work over a very long time. But did they have a long time was the question.

"*Star Mist*, would you please show a blue dome beyond all these galaxies illustrated?"

A blue dome, vast in size appeared beyond the hundreds of thousands of galaxies.

"Our third line of defense and why we need extreme long-range scanners. If any of their ships move past those galaxies or get out like that first ship that started all this, we need to have sensors out there that spot it."

Gage felt that would work and so did everyone else. But they were talking hundreds and hundreds of years, if not thousands.

"We are assuming these aliens are all going in one general direction," Angie said, bringing back up what *Star Mist* had mentioned. "We need to scout to see if there are more fronts on this battle besides this one."

"Agreed," Benny said.

Gage hated that, but he knew Angie was right and they didn't have enough information to know if this alien plague was spreading in only one general direction or in a complete circle. They basically only had the data they had gotten from the other human groups.

"Are we agreed on this plan in general?" Angie asked.

Every chairman in the room nodded.

"So what do we do about the other human groups?" Gage asked. He had no idea on this problem.

He looked around. Silence greeted him.

So Gage looked at Ray and Tacita directly. "Your suggestions? These two groups are clearly from your past and I would assume there is still bad blood."

Ray nodded and Tacita said nothing.

"Would they be worth our time in bringing them into this plan," Benny asked. "Their ships are no faster than the alien ships?"

Gage could see nothing but problems with even contacting them, but he said nothing.

"We let them do what they are doing," Angie said.

"I agree," Benny said.

"We don't hide from them," Carey said.

"No hiding," Matt said, nodding.

"Damn right no hiding," Benny said. "We're out here cleaning up their mess. They started all this. Screw them."

Ray and Tacita both nodded and both looked slightly relieved.

"All right," Angie said. "One more thing. How about we set up some major ship factories in galaxies on that third line of defense?"

She looked at Tacita and Ray. "How fast could a major ship factory be set up on a planet on that third line of defense and how many large military craft could be built that would carry a hundred of the small fighters?"

"In essence," Gage said. "We are thinking small military mother ships to repair, transport, and so on."

"We will have that answer for you in one day," Ray said and Tacita nodded.

"That is a very good idea," Tacita said.

"Not one ship can get through," Carey said. "We all need to remember that."

"And we all need to brief our entire crews on what is happening," Gage said.

"We do it at the same time twelve hours from now," Gina said.

"They all agreed.

"Let's get started," Angie said.

Gage looked directly at Ray and Tacita as they stood. "We need that extreme long-range scanner and we need it quickly."

Both nodded.

"And I have a hunch," Gage said, "if we are going to save humanity from its stupid mistake this time, every resource we have, not only from the Milky Way, but already Seeded galaxies will be needed in the fight."

Both again nodded.

"We will get every resource we can think of moving in this direction," Ray said.

He took Tacita's hand and they both vanished.

Gage glanced at Angie and she just nodded.

The decision had been made, but Gage knew it actually hadn't been a decision. A group of humans had made a mistake and their creation had gotten lose. Now for the sake of the known human universe, that mistake had to be stopped.

Gage hated that, but he knew it had to be done, no matter how long it took.

And he had no doubt this coming fight was going to take a very, very long time.

Centuries. But at the moment, he just couldn't think that far ahead.

CHAPTER 39

For three solid days, the six chairmen worked and planned morning, noon and night, until it finally became clear to all of them that this fight was going to take years, decades, maybe even longer. Such a long time that Angie had a tough time even imagining.

And until someone invented a long-range scanner, they didn't even have any idea if they were winning or losing the fight. And Ray had told them it might take a decade for that breakthrough.

She wasn't sure if they had a decade, but they would do their best.

The weight of all this rested on the six of them. And Angie felt it every day. The image of how the aliens spread over the Milky Way galaxy haunted her night and day.

It was after a long meeting of the eight chairmen that Gage suggested to Angie they go to their quarters. He had mentioned to her that they needed to start getting into regular eating and sleeping routines and she had agreed. But so far, it hadn't been possible.

When they arrived, Angie was surprised to see that the table had been set with candles and dinner was staying warm in the oven. It smelled heavenly, like a fine Italian pasta and garlic bread.

"When did you have time to do this, mister?" she asked, turning to smile at Gage.

He laughed. "I asked for a little help from Soma and one of the ship's chefs."

Angie kissed him.

"We're staying in here for the evening," Gage said, smiling at her as he escorted her to her chair. "The known universe will have to get along without us for a short time."

She smiled as he put the wonderful-smelling pasta on the table and the garlic bread and then took his spot across from her.

In the living room, Miss Star, one of their now four cats noticed the food and got down from the back of the couch and came over beside the table.

Angie just stared at Gage's handsome beaming face and his wonderful green eyes. She never had gotten tired of doing that.

"So what's the occasion?" she asked

He pointed to the food. "Already forgotten our first meal together?"

She laughed, the memory of that first evening together in Portland flooding back in as clear as if had happened yesterday.

They had eaten exactly this same meal.

"Happy fifteen years from that first date," he said.

That surprised her. Had fifteen years really gone by? Wow, just wow.

He came around kissed her and she kissed him back.

No matter what was happening outside this apartment, they

had each other and for that she couldn't be more grateful and happy.

Finally, before either of them broke their resolve and headed for the bedroom, Gage went back to his chair and they both dug into the food.

It was heavenly.

And just like the first night, the conversation over the food was fun and light and about anything but the fight with the alien expansion.

As they did on that first night, they ended up making passionate love after dinner.

Even after fifteen years, it was better than the first night.

She couldn't believe she had been with this wonderful man for that many years. Her memory was so clear of those first few days together, they seemed like yesterday.

And she remembered clearly that both of them had worried about their abilities to keep a long-term relationship going.

She could understand fifteen years. She wasn't sure about centuries, but she had a hunch the two of them would take that one year at a time.

But long term sure didn't seem like a problem anymore for either of them.

And as they lay there, holding each other, they talked about the wonderful fifteen years and their hope for far more than that.

Two cats joined them on the foot of the bed, wondering what she and Gage were doing, but not jumping down.

Gage mentioned how fast the years had passed and how happy he was and she agreed, adding in how happy she was that she wasn't aging.

And they laughed about how worried they both had been about a lasting relationship. It seemed so ironic to her now.

Finally, Angie turned and kissed him, then said, "Thank you?"

"The sex was that good?" he asked, pretending to be shocked.

She laughed. "Yes, thank you for that, but thank you more for this wonderful surprise evening and remembering our first night. I needed to be reminded why we are here doing what we are doing."

He nodded, then said simply, "I needed the reminder as well."

"So, let's make sure we mark every year with something special," she said.

"To keep us grounded."

"Grounded in a spaceship with over a million people under our command," she said, smiling. "Yeah, that kind of grounded."

He laughed and just shook his head to that.

After a moment, she raised up and looked at him. "If memory serves, which it does just fine, we made love twice that first night."

"That was pure sex," he said. "I fell in love with you long before that night following you around in the wilds of the mountains."

She laughed and agreed that the first night had been wonderful, pure passionate sex.

"So lieutenant, are you up for a second round this evening?" she asked after a moment.

"You know I'm over four hundred years old, don't you?" he said, looking into her eyes.

"So I take that as a yes," she said, looking into his deep green eyes.

"Hell, yes," he said.

And she giggled like a young girl as he moved toward her, scattering cats to the floor.

And for the first time in years, she felt young again.

If you enjoyed *Star Mist*, try the next thrilling novel in the Seeders Universe series, *Star Rain*! What follows is a sample chapter.

PROLOGUE

(Twenty-seven years before the discovery of the aliens…)

The last three years had gone faster than Chairman Evan West had expected. Around him on the command center of the *Rescue One,* the fifteen members of his main crew were all standing ready at their stations on the three levels, all scanning ahead as much as they could.

He knew that through the entire ship the thirty thousand people on board were also watching intently.

West was a tall, thin man with bright green eyes, balding head, and wide shoulders. People said he had a smile that made him a lot of friends and he liked to laugh and have fun.

Lately he hadn't smiled much.

The air was tense in the large room around him, but professional. The large screen that filled the tall wall in front of them only showed the quickly approaching front edge of the small galaxy they were calling Destination. The galaxy had a number, but no one called it by that anymore.

West stood beside his large chairman's chair, watching not only his instruments, but those of his second and third in command at their stations on either side of him.

Nothing.

Just nothing out of the ordinary at all.

They were on a mission to find out what had happened to the *Dreaming Large,* one of the huge Seeder mother ships. It had vanished in the small galaxy they were now approaching.

That had been four years ago, a short time for a Seeder, but a very long time for a major mother ship to vanish completely.

Mother ships were the size of large moons and built to look like a giant bird in flight. A mother ship could hold a few thousand smaller ships and upward of a million or more people. It was from the mother ships that Seeders spread humanity from one galaxy to another, always moving forward.

Chairman West had been a seeder now for three thousand years and had seen many galaxies along the way. And he had helped in birthing more billions of human societies than he wanted to even try to imagine.

He loved his job.

He didn't much like this mission.

His wife and best friend, Tammy, had been on the *Dreaming Large* when it vanished. He missed their nightly routines of telling each other their days through a trans-tunnel link, even when they had been apart for years. He loved her and always had loved her. They had been a team for centuries.

And he missed her now more than he wanted to ever admit.

Their plan had been for him to finish up the last part of a

seeding mission in the previous galaxy and then his ship and a dozen other front-line ships with him would catch up with the *Dreaming Large*. He liked working the front edge of the seeding as he always did after the terraforming was finished.

He had worried for the three years it took them at full trans-tunnel speed to get here and he had missed Tammy every moment of it. He had no idea what they were going to find. No one had an idea, even though the speculation was rampart.

How could a major Seeder mother ship simply vanish?

Without a word of notice, the two chairmen who jointly ran the mother ship had stopped reporting in to Chairman Ray.

When that had happened, Chairman Ray had contacted him and the idea of *Rescue One* was born.

There were twenty-two mother ships now, built over centuries, with more being built all the time. The *Dreaming Large* was the first to vanish.

Tammy had been one of the head botanists on *Dreaming Large*. She had loved her job, just as he loved his.

The *Rescue One* had been built especially for this mission.

Unlike most Seeders' ships, the *Rescue One* had a full military contingent and four warships on board, commanded by West's best friend, Ben Cline. Seeders, by their very mission and scouting ahead, never had much need for military until some of the growing new human cultures hit their early space age stage. So to even put together a military fleet, Cline had scrounged through some more advanced human cultures recently seeded for ships and enough new Seeders to man the ships.

It had taken Cline as long to put his force together as it had to build the *Rescue One*.

The *Rescue One* had been built in preparation for almost anything they might find. It also had in its huge hangar twenty of the Seeders' fastest scout ships, all crewed with upward of twenty thousand people each and ready to go.

And it had room, if necessary, for a hundred thousand survivors, a fraction of the humans who had been on the *Dreaming Large* when it vanished.

Now, finally, after the year of building and three years of travel at the fastest trans-tunnel speeds any Seeder ship could go, they were almost there.

"Anything?" West asked, breaking the silence on the large command center and glancing around the three levels at his first shift crew.

All of them shook their heads.

"Full stop at scouting distance from the edge of Destination," he ordered.

"We'll be at full stop in one minute," Korgan said.

Korgan was his second in command and had been chairman of his own scout ship before volunteering to go on this mission. He had family, a son and a daughter, on the *Dreaming Large*.

In fact, a good third of the crew of the *Rescue One* had family or some personal connection to crew on the *Dreaming Large*.

That made this crew very, very motivated to find the lost mother ship.

"Dropping out of trans-warp now," Korgan said, his voice seeming to almost echo in the silence of the large bridge.

"Full scans," West said.

Then he motioned to Korgan to have the crews of the scout ships stand ready and be scanning as well.

West moved over and stood beside his command chair. He couldn't make himself sit in the chair until they knew what had happened to *Dreaming Large*. But from where he stood, he could see all the data streaming in.

Destination was a small spiral galaxy on the scheme of things, with about 80 billion stars of all standard sizes. It showed no unusual areas at all.

And not a sign of the *Dreaming Large*.

Nothing.

The huge mother ship had just vanished.

West left his chairman's chair after a few minutes and walked slowly around to all the stations on his bridge, not so much for information, but to give everyone some time and let himself relax a little.

He had been preparing for this moment for four years. Rushing anything now might lead to even more problems.

Finally, after the longest half hour he had ever spent in the command center, he broke the intense silence.

"Let's have some reports," he said. "So everyone can be together on this. And broadcast these reports to the entire ship please."

Korgan nodded for West to go ahead.

"Anything unusual at all about Destination?"

Three stations reported in that there was nothing unusual. Then Korgan added. "What we are reading matches exactly the last reports of the scout ships two hundred years before the *Dreaming Large* arrived here."

West nodded. "Any signs of alien or human habitation?"

Six reports came in quickly, one after another, cutting the small galaxy down into six quadrants, just as it would have been seeded.

Nothing.

No alien life, no human life, no remains of any ship anywhere.

As with most galaxies, this one was empty. And if it had an alien race at any level anywhere in the galaxy, the entire galaxy would have just been left alone and the *Dreaming Large* would have gone on to the next empty galaxy.

Not one sign that the *Dreaming Large* had even started terraforming the Goldilocks zone planets around yellow stars. Whatever had happened, it had happened before the *Dreaming Large* entered Destination.

"More information as we have it," West said, signaling to Korgan to cut the communication to the entire ship.

West did one more walk around the bridge, looking at details on a few reports, but finding nothing different at all.

Finally, he went down to stand near his station.

"*Rescue One*," he said, "please put on the screen a two-dimensional representation of the galaxies closest to Destination. Limit the galaxies to a one-year travel time for the *Dreaming Large* from this point."

Thirty-one galaxies came up, represented as dots. There were a couple clusters and ten galaxies seemed to have formed a group. Over the last three years he had stared at this very map more than he wanted to admit.

But he knew that the *Dreaming Large* would not have gone to any of those other galaxies without reporting in. And with Destination being an empty galaxy, perfect for seeding, there would have been no reason to move on.

This was exactly what he had feared. What Chairman Ray had also feared.

"Now, *Rescue One*," West said to his ship, "please add into the scanning equipment the ability to see pockets of empty space."

Everyone on the bridge crew just stopped and looked at him like he had lost a marble or two.

Almost no one had heard of empty space. He hadn't either until this mission started.

West had been briefed by Chairman Ray and his wife, Chairman Tacita, on the very reality of empty space, or void space as it was sometimes called.

Basically, empty space was a very small bubble in space, often not more than the size of a standard solar system, where space was completely empty and time and the rules of physics did not apply for some reason inside it.

Over the centuries, Seeder ships had just vanished when they ran into a bubble of empty space.

And they would often emerge thousands, if not hundreds of thousands of years later having only spent less than a shipboard few hours in empty space.

Chairman Ray had warned West that if there were no logical reasons for *Dreaming Large* to have vanished, no signs of any debris, or any human survivors, then West was to look for empty space pockets.

The scientists on some of the more advanced Seeder ships had developed a program to show complete emptiness, something normal space did not have.

It had taken the scientists three years of frantic work to finally develop and test the long-range scanning program.

And if this worked, every Seeder ship would get the program as an update and hopefully no more ships would be lost to centuries in an empty space bubble.

For the year that the scanning program had been uploaded to *Rescue One*, the scientists had continued to make adjustments and sent them along. West had told no one about any of it.

"Loaded," *Rescue One* said.

"Display on the screen as dots the empty space areas within four galaxies radius of this location," West said.

Then red dots appeared. Only about eight total in that much space, but one was seemingly right where they were.

They were within brushing distance of the edge of an empty space bubble.

"Shit!' West said. "Back us away from the edge of that thing to a distance of two light years."

West couldn't believe that they had almost vanished right into empty space as well.

That had been far, far too close.

"We're back away from it," Korgan reported a few long moments later. "What exactly is empty space?"

"That's where the *Dreaming Large* is trapped," West said.

The big mother ship had to be right here very close to them, only stuck in a bubble of no time and space. And the mother ship might not emerge for a hundred thousand years.

All West could see in his mind was the smiling face of his wife.

Somehow, they had to rescue the big ship, even though, more than likely, no one on the big ship even knew anything was wrong yet.

But he and *Rescue One* and its crew had to pull off the impossible and get *Dreaming Large* out of there.

Somehow.

Over the next five years, the *Rescue One* went from a military-based rescue operation to a full-fledged science ship. West had remained as chairman on request, a request that Chairman Ray had gladly granted.

And Chairman Ray had put West in charge of the overall mission. All ships' chairmen in the area reported to him.

Entire parts of *Rescue One* were being reconfigured into research labs to study the empty space bubble holding the *Dreaming Large* mother ship.

Admiral Cline had taken all his military ships and headed back to help out at the last seeded galaxy with upcoming wars between developing human planets.

The fleet of scout ships they had brought with them all scattered out to do what they do, scout ahead, map galaxies and spot trouble galaxies that had the occasional growing alien race.

Almost every day another science ship arrived at *Rescue One* and took a location either in space near *Rescue One* or on one of the large decks where the military ships and scout ships had once been housed.

Almost fifty smaller science ships had now surrounded the small bubble of empty space, studying it, trying to see inside it.

Every Seeder's ship now had the scanning ability to see and avoid empty space bubbles, something that West had no doubt would save ships from losing thousands and thousands of years.

Now they just had to figure out a way to get the *Dreaming Large* out of there in under a few thousand years.

Every day Chairman West had a meeting with the four top science advisors to get reports on any progress. They usually met for breakfast in his own kitchen in his apartment, taking turns cooking and cleaning and talking about the problem.

All four were chairmen of their own major science ships.

It was right before one meeting that West came up with an idea. He had been sitting at his kitchen counter, staring at a surface rendering of the patterns on the border of the empty space and he suddenly saw it a different way.

They had been working to find a way to shield themselves from the effects of the empty space, go in and shield *Dreaming*

Large as well. What would happen if they just drained the empty space out into normal space?

Or better yet, filled empty space with normal space.

In essence, they needed to pop the bubble, leaving the *Dreaming Large* surprised at all the company it suddenly had around it.

The four scientists loved that idea and after the meeting, West contacted Chairman Ray and told him about it to get scientists in numbers of galaxies working on the problem as well.

It took seven more years to find the solution.

Seven very long and frustrating years.

Now West stood in the command center of the *Rescue One* yet again, sixteen years after he had agreed to join this project, ready to try to finally release *Dreaming Large.*

As everyone had been warned, no one on *Dreaming Large* would even realize they had been in trouble. As far as those on board the giant mother ship knew, only a few seconds had transpired since they entered empty space and their trans-tunnel drives had suddenly shut down.

If what *Rescue One* and all the other ships were about to do worked, the hundreds and hundreds of ships that now swarmed the area would suddenly just appear to those on *Dreaming Large.*

If it worked.

And if the forces didn't pull *Dreaming Large* apart.

Chairman Ray and others had said that the giant mother ships were designed to withstand plowing into planets and going right on through. Ray wasn't worried about that at all.

But West was.

They had calculated the trajectory where *Dreaming Large* had entered the empty space bubble and cleared every ship out of the way where it would be headed.

What they were going to try to do was in essence take the pressure of empty space away by opening not just one, but thousands of holes in it all at once. Just as firefighters did to a burning structure under pressure. They opened many outlets instead of just one.

The scientists a few years back had determined exactly what strange gravitational force was holding empty space together like a bubble, allowing a ship to enter and leave, yet holding the space together.

And once they had determined that force, they knew how to puncture the force to not so much let empty space out, but to let regular space and time flood in.

The entire bubble should, the scientists had told West, just vanish as if it had never existed.

West could only hope.

"Report status," West said to all the ships around the bubble ready to send a hundred probes each to open up holes.

A moment later Korgan looked up at him and nodded. "All eighty ships report green, Chairman."

West nodded, staring at the big screen in front of him showing nothing but empty space.

"Mission go," West said.

West knew that once he said that, a computer program from *Rescue One* would launch all probes at the exact same moment from all ships.

West had been told that the probes would have a small charge when they hit the membrane, so it would look like eight thousand tiny lights flashing at the same time in a sphere shape in open space.

"Five seconds," Korgan said.

Intense, heavy silence filled the bridge of the ship.

West had no doubt not one word was being said anywhere in the large fleet of ships surrounding the empty space bubble.

West could not for a second take his gaze away from the massive screen in front of him.

Suddenly, there was a white flash of light from what looked like the surface of a sphere.

Then a moment later, the massive mother ship *Dreaming Large* appeared.

Cheering erupted around the bridge.

West just stood there grinning, staring at the screen, knowing that finally, after sixteen years, he would finally get to see his wife's face again. And maybe a little later actually hug her and kiss her.

After a moment, Korgan, a smile almost splitting his face, turned to West. "I have the two chairmen of the *Dreaming Large* asking just what the hell is going on."

West just smiled right back at Korgan. "Tell them to contact Chairman Ray and let him explain."

Then, for seemingly the first time in sixteen years, he went and sat down in his chairman's chair.

And then on a private channel he said to *Rescue One*, "Please contact my wife on *Dreaming Large* and put her through to my personal screen here."

"I will be glad to, Chairman," *Rescue One* said.

"Thank you," he said.

And then, for the first time in sixteen years, he took a deep breath and relaxed.

NEWSLETTER SIGN-UP

Follow Dean on BookBub

Be the first to know!

Just sign up for the Dean Wesley Smith newsletter, and keep up with the latest news, releases and so much more—even the occasional giveaway.
So, what are you waiting for? To sign up go to deanwesleysmith.com.

But wait! There's more. Sign up for the WMG Publishing newsletter, too, and get the latest news and releases from all of the WMG authors and lines, including Kristine Kathryn Rusch, Kristine Grayson, Kris Nelscott, *Pulphouse Fiction Magazine, Smith's Monthly,* and so much more.
To sign up go to wmgpublishing.com.

ABOUT THE AUTHOR

Considered one of the most prolific writers working in modern fiction, *USA Today* bestselling writer Dean Wesley Smith published far more than a hundred novels in forty years, and hundreds of short stories across many genres.

At the moment he produces novels in several major series, including the time travel Thunder Mountain novels set in the Old West, the galaxy-spanning Seeders Universe series, the urban fantasy Ghost of a Chance series, a superhero series starring Poker Boy, and a mystery series featuring the retired detectives of the Cold Poker Gang.

His monthly magazine, *Smith's Monthly*, which consists of only his own fiction, premiered in October 2013 and offers readers more than 70,000 words per issue, including a new and original novel every month.

During his career, Dean also wrote a couple dozen *Star Trek* novels, the only two original *Men in Black* novels, Spider-Man and X-Men novels, plus novels set in gaming and television worlds. Writing with his wife Kristine Kathryn Rusch under the name Kathryn Wesley, he wrote the novel for the NBC miniseries The Tenth Kingdom and other books for *Hallmark Hall of Fame* movies.

He wrote novels under dozens of pen names in the worlds of comic books and movies, including novelizations of almost a dozen films, from *The Final Fantasy* to *Steel* to *Rundown*.

Dean also worked as a fiction editor off and on, starting at Pulphouse Publishing, then at *VB Tech Journal*, then Pocket Books, and now at WMG Publishing, where he and Kristine Kathryn Rusch serve as series editors for the acclaimed *Fiction River* anthology series.

For more information about Dean's books and ongoing projects, please visit his website at www.deanwesleysmith.com and sign up for his newsletter.

For more information:
www.deanwesleysmith.com

facebook.com/deanwsmith3
twitter.com/deanwesleysmith